Arthur Hugh Clough

Selections from the Poems of Arthur Hugh Clough

Arthur Hugh Clough

Selections from the Poems of Arthur Hugh Clough

ISBN/EAN: 9783744764728

Printed in Europe, USA, Canada, Australia, Japan

Cover: Foto ©Andreas Hilbeck / pixelio.de

More available books at **www.hansebooks.com**

SELECTIONS FROM THE POEMS

OF

ARTHUR HUGH CLOUGH

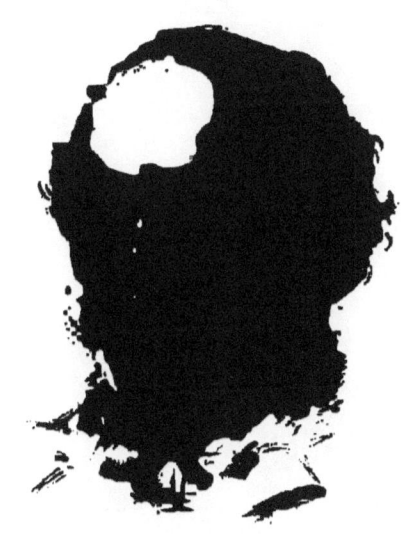

Engraved by C. H. Jeens

𝕷𝖔𝖓𝖉𝖔𝖓

MACMILLAN AND CO.

AND NEW YORK

1894

PREFACE

THE poems by Arthur Hugh Clough given in
this selection are placed in order of time, except
the "Bothie," which, written in 1848, at the
moment of his leaving Oxford, should chron-
ologically have followed the Early Poems.
These were written between 1837 and 1847,
between the ages of nineteen and twenty-nine,
and correspond with his life at Oxford as Under-
graduate, Fellow, and Tutor. "Dipsychus" and
the "Amours de Voyage" were written in 1849
and 1850, called forth by Italian journeys made
during his three years' residence in London.

The Miscellaneous Poems also belong to this
time, except the Sea Songs, which were written
during his voyage to America in 1852. "Come,
Poet, Come!" also belongs to a later time.

After his return to England in 1853, when
he entered the Education Office, he wrote no
more during the last eight years of his life till

the last year, when the enforced leisure caused
by ill health seemed to renew in him the
creative impulse.   Among other things he
then produced the group of poems called
" Mari Magno."   These, however, are not re-
presented here, not seeming well adapted for
selections.   In 1861 he died, aged forty-two,
leaving us to wonder what might have come
later had longer life been granted him.

B. M. S. C.

March 1894.

CONTENTS

THE

BOTHIE OF TOBER-NA-VUOLICH:

A LONG-VACATION PASTORAL

Nunc formosissimus annus
Ite meæ felix quondam pecus, ite camenæ

THE BOTHIE OF TOBER-NA-VUOLICH

I

Socii cratera coronant

IT was the afternoon ; and the sports were now at
    the ending.
Long had the stone been put, tree cast, and
    thrown the hammer ;
Up the perpendicular hill, Sir Hector so called it,
Eight stout gillies had run, with speed and agility
    wondrous ;
Run too the course on the level had been ; the
    leaping was over :
Last in the show of dress, a novelty recently
    added,
Noble ladies their prizes adjudged for costume
    that was perfect,
Turning the clansmen about, as they stood with
    upraised elbows ;
Bowing their eye-glassed brows, and fingering
    kilt and sporran.
It was four of the clock, and the sports were come
    to the ending,
Therefore the Oxford party went off to adorn for
    the dinner.

Be it recorded in song who was first, who last,
in dressing.
Hope was first, black-tied, white-waistcoated,
simple, His Honour ;
For the postman made out he was heir to the
earldom of Ilay
(Being the younger son of the younger brother,
the Colonel),
Treated him therefore with special respect ; doffed
bonnet, and ever
Called him His Honour ; His Honour he therefore
was at the cottage ;
Always His Honour at least, sometimes the Vis-
count of Ilay.
  Hope was first, His Honour, and next to His
. Honour the Tutor.
Still more plain the Tutor, the grave man, nick-
named Adam,
White-tied, clerical, silent, with antique square-
cut waistcoat
Formal, unchanged, of black cloth, but with sense
and feeling beneath it ;
Skilful in Ethics and Logic, in Pindar and Poets
unrivalled ;
Shady in Latin, said Lindsay, but *topping* in Plays
and Aldrich.
  Somewhat more splendid in dress, in a waist-
coat work of a lady,
Lindsay succeeded ; the lively, the cheery, cigar-
loving Lindsay,
Lindsay the ready of speech, the Piper, the
Dialectician,

This was his title from Adam because of the
    words he invented,
Who in three weeks had created a dialect new for
    the party ;
This was his title from Adam, but mostly they
    called him the Piper.
Lindsay succeeded, the lively, the cheery, cigar-
    loving Lindsay.
    Hewson and Hobbes were down at the *matutine*
    bathing ; of course too
Arthur, the bather of bathers, *par excellence*,
    Audley by surname,
Arthur they called him for love and for euphony ;
    they had been bathing,
Where in the morning was custom, where over a
    ledge of granite
Into a granite basin the amber torrent descended,
Only a step from the cottage, the road and larches
    between them.
Hewson and Hobbes followed quick upon Adam ;
    on them followed Arthur.
    Airlie descended the last, effulgent as god of
    Olympus ;
Blue, perceptibly blue, was the coat that had
    white silk facings,
Waistcoat blue, coral-buttoned, the white tie finely
    adjusted,
Coral moreover the studs on a shirt as of crochet
    of women :
When the fourwheel for ten minutes already had
    stood at the gateway,
He, like a god, came leaving his ample Olympian
    chamber.

And in the fourwheel they drove to the place of
the clansmen's meeting.
So in the fourwheel they came ; and Donald
the innkeeper showed them
Up to the barn where the dinner should be.   Four
tables were in it ;
Two at the top and the bottom, a little upraised
from the level,
These for Chairman and Croupier, and gentry fit
to be with them,
Two lengthways in the midst for keeper and gillie
and peasant.
Here were clansmen many in kilt and bonnet
assembled,
Keepers a dozen at least ; the Marquis's targeted
gillies ;
Pipers five or six, among them the young one, the
drunkard ;
Many with silver brooches, and some with those
brilliant crystals
Found amid granite-dust on the frosty scalp of the
Cairn-Gorm ;
But with snuff-boxes all, and all of them using the
boxes.
Here too were Catholic Priest, and Established
Minister standing :
Catholic Priest ; for many still clung to the Ancient
Worship,
And Sir Hector's father himself had built them a
chapel ;
So stood Priest and Minister, near to each other,
but silent,
One to say grace before, the other after the dinner.

Hither anon too came the shrewd, ever-ciphering
    Factor,
Hither anon the Attaché, the Guardsman mute
    and stately,
Hither from lodge and bothie in all the adjoining
    shootings
Members of Parliament many, forgetful of votes
    and bluebooks,
Here, amid heathery hills, upon beast and bird of
    the forest
Venting the murderous spleen of the endless
    Railway Committee.
Hither the Marquis of Ayr, and Dalgarnish Earl
    and Croupier,
And at their side, amid murmurs of welcome, long
    looked-for, himself too
Eager, the grey, but boy-hearted Sir Hector, the
    Chief and the Chairman.   ·
    Then was the dinner served, and the Minister
    prayed for a blessing,
And to the viands before them with knife and with
    fork they beset them :
Venison, the red and the roe, with mutton ; and
    grouse succeeding ;
Such was the feast, with whisky of course, and
    at top and bottom
Small decanters of sherry, not overchoice, for the
    gentry.
So to the viands before them with laughter and
    chat they beset them.
And, when on flesh and on fowl had appetite duly
    been sated.

Up rose the Catholic Priest and returned God
    thanks for the dinner.
Then on all tables were set black bottles of well-
    mixed toddy,
And, with the bottles and glasses before them,
    they sat, digesting,
Talking, enjoying, but chiefly awaiting the toasts
    and speeches.

  Spare me, O great Recollection! for words to
    the task were unequal,
Spare me, O mistress of Song! nor bid me
    remember minutely
All that was said and done o'er the well-mixed
    tempting toddy ;
How were healths proposed and drunk ' with all
    the honours,'
Glasses and bonnets waving, and three-times-three
    thrice over,
Queen, and Prince, and Army, and Landlords all,
    and Keepers ;
Bid me not, grammar defying, repeat from
    grammar-defiers
Long constructions strange and plusquam-Thucy-
    didean ;
Tell how, as sudden torrent in time of speat [1] in
    the mountain
Hurries six ways at once, and takes at last to the
    roughest,
Or as the practised rider at Astley's or Franconi's
Skilfully, boldly bestrides many steeds at once in
    the gallop,

          [1] Flood.

Crossing from this to that, with one leg here, one
    yonder,
So, less skilful, but equally bold, and wild as the
    torrent,
All through sentences six at a time, unsuspecting
    of syntax,
Hurried the lively good-will and garrulous tale of
    Sir Hector.
Left to oblivion be it, the memory, faithful as
    ever,
How the Marquis of Ayr, with wonderful gesticula-
    tion,
Floundering on through game and mess-room
    recollections,
Gossip of neighbouring forest, praise of targeted
    gillies,
Anticipation of royal visit, skits at pedestrians,
Swore he would never abandon his country, nor
    give up deer-stalking ;
How, too, more brief, and plainer, in spite of the
    Gaelic accent,
Highland peasants gave courteous answer to
    flattering nobles.
Two orations alone the memorial song will
    render ;
For at the banquet's close spake thus the lively
    Sir Hector,
Somewhat husky with praises exuberant, often
    repeated,
Pleasant to him and to them, of the gallant
    Highland soldiers
Whom he erst led in the fight ;—something husky,
    but ready, though weary,

Up to them rose and spoke the grey but gladsome
    chieftain :—
    Fill up your glasses, my friends, once more,—
    With all the honours !
There was a toast I forgot, which our gallant
    Highland homes have
Always welcomed the stranger, delighted, I may
    say, to see such
Fine young men at my table—My friends ! are you
    ready ? the Strangers.
Gentlemen, here are your healths,—and I wish you
    —With all the honours !
So he said, and the cheers ensued, and all the
    honours,
All our Collegians were bowed to, the Attaché
    detecting His Honour,
Guardsman moving to Arthur, and Marquis sidling
    to Airlie,
And the small Piper below getting up and nodding
    to Lindsay.
    But, while the healths were being drunk, was
    much tribulation and trouble,
Nodding and beckoning across, observed of
    Attaché and Guardsman :
Adam wouldn't speak,—indeed it was certain he
    couldn't ;
Hewson could, and would if they wished ; Philip
    Hewson a poet,
Hewson a radical hot, hating lords and scorning
    ladies,
Silent mostly, but often reviling in fire and fury
Feudal tenures, mercantile lords, competition and
    bishops,

Liveries, armorial bearings, amongst other matters
    the Game-laws :
He could speak, and was asked to by Adam ; but
    Lindsay aloud cried,
(Whisky was hot in his brain), Confound it, no,
    not Hewson,
Ain't he cock-sure to bring in his eternal political
    humbug ?
However, so it must be, and after due pause of
    silence,
Waving his hand to Lindsay, and smiling oddly
    to Adam,
Up to them rose and spoke the poet and radical
    Hewson :—
   I am, I think, perhaps the most perfect stranger
    present.
I have not, as have some of my friends, in my
    veins some tincture,
Some few ounces of Scottish blood ; no, nothing
    like it.
I am therefore perhaps the fittest to answer and
    thank you.
So I thank you, sir, for myself and for my com-
    panions,
Heartily thank you all for this unexpected greeting,
All the more welcome, as showing you do not
    account us intruders,
Are not unwilling to see the north and the south
    forgather.
And, surely, seldom have Scotch and English
    more thoroughly mingled ;
Scarcely with warmer hearts, and clearer feeling
    of manhood,

Even in tourney, and foray, and fray, and regular
 battle,
Where the life and the strength came out in the
 tug and tussle,
Scarcely, where man met man, and soul encoun-
 tered with soul, as
Close as do the bodies and twining limbs of the
 wrestlers,
When for a final bout are a day's two champions
 mated,—
In the grand old times of bows, and bills, and
 claymores,
At the old Flodden-field—or Bannockburn—or
 Culloden.
—(And he paused a moment, for breath, and
 because of some cheering)
We are the better friends, I fancy, for that old
 fighting,
Better friends, inasmuch as we know each other
 the better,
We can now shake hands without pretending or
 shuffling.
On this passage followed a great tornado of
 cheering,
Tables were rapped, feet stamped, a glass or two
 got broken :
He, ere the cheers died wholly away, and while
 still there was stamping,
Added, in altered voice, with a smile, his doubtful
 conclusion.
 I have, however, less claim than others perhaps
 to this honour,

For, let me say, I am neither game-keeper, nor
  game-preserver.
  So he said, and sat down, but his satire had
  not been taken.
Only the *men*, who were all on their legs as con-
  cerned in the thanking,
Were a trifle confused, but mostly sat down with-
  out laughing ;
Lindsay alone, close-facing the chair, shook his
  fist at the speaker.
Only a Liberal member, away at the end of the table,
Started, remembering sadly the cry of a coming
  election,
Only the Attaché glanced at the Guardsman, who
  twirled his moustachio,
Only the Marquis faced round, but, not quite clear
  of the meaning,
Joined with the joyous Sir Hector, who lustily beat
  on the table.
  And soon after the chairman arose, and the
  feast was over :
Now should the barn be cleared and forthwith
  adorned for the dancing,
And, to make way for this purpose, the Tutor and
  pupils retiring
Were by the chieftain addressed and invited to
  come to the castle.
But ere the door-way they quitted, a thin man
  clad as the Saxon,
Trouser and cap and jacket of homespun blue,
  hand-woven,
Singled out, and said with determined accent, to
  Hewson,

Touching his arm : Young man, if ye pass through
the Braes o' Lochaber,
See by the loch-side ye come to the Bothie of
Tober-na-vuolich.

II

Et certamen erat, Corydon cum Thyrside, magnum

MORN, in yellow and white, came broadening out
from the mountains,
Long ere music and reel were hushed in the barn
of the dancers.
Duly in *matutine* bathed, before eight some two
of the party,
Where in the morning was custom, where over a
ledge of granite
Into a granite basin the amber torrent descended.
There two plunges each took Philip and Arthur
together,
Duly in *matutine* bathed, and read, and waited
for breakfast :
Breakfast commencing at nine, lingered lazily on
to noon-day.
Tea and coffee were there; a jug of water for
Hewson ;
Tea and coffee; and four cold grouse upon the
sideboard ;
Gaily they talked, as they sat, some late and lazy
at breakfast,
Some professing a book, some smoking outside
at the window.

By an aurora soft-pouring a still sheeny tide to
    the zenith,
Hewson and Arthur, with Adam, had walked and
    got home by eleven ;
Hope and the others had stayed till the round sun
    lighted them bedward.
They of the lovely aurora, but these of the lovelier
    women
Spoke—of noble ladies and rustic girls, their
    partners.
  Turned to them Hewson, the Chartist, the poet,
    the eloquent speaker.
Sick of the very names of your Lady Augustas
    and Floras
Am I, as ever I was of the dreary botanical
    titles
Of the exotic plants, their antitypes in the hot-
    house :
Roses, violets, lilies for me ! the out-of-door
    beauties ;
Meadow and woodland sweets, forget-me-nots and
    heart's-ease !
  Pausing awhile, he proceeded anon, for none
    made answer.
Oh, if our high-born girls knew only the grace,
    the attraction,
Labour, and labour alone, can add to the beauty
    of women,
Truly the milliner's trade would quickly, I think,
    be at discount,
All the waste and loss in silk and satin be saved
    us,

Saved for purposes truly and widely produc-
    tive——

                       That's right,
Take off your coat to it, Philip, cried Lindsay,
    outside in the garden,
Take off your coat to it, Philip.
           Well, then, said Hewson, resuming ;
Laugh if you please at my novel economy ; listen
    to this, though ;
As for myself, and apart from economy wholly,
    believe me,
Never I properly felt the relation between men
    and women,
Though to the dancing-master I went perforce,
    for a quarter,
Where, in dismal quadrille, were good-looking girls
    in abundance,
Though, too, school-girl cousins were mine—a
    bevy of beauties—
Never (of course you will laugh, but of course all
    the same I shall say it),
Never, believe me, I knew of the feelings between
    men and women,
Till in some village fields in holidays now getting
    stupid,
One day sauntering 'long and listless,' as Tenny-
    son has it,
Long and listless strolling, ungainly in hobbadiboy-
    hood,
Chanced it my eye fell aside on a capless, bonnetless
    maiden,
Bending with three-pronged fork in a garden
    uprooting potatoes.

Was it the air? who can say? or herself, or the
    charm of the labour?
But a new thing was in me; and longing delicious
    possessed me,
Longing to take her and lift her, and put her
    away from her slaving.
Was it embracing or aiding was most in my mind?
    hard question!
But a new thing was in me; I, too, was a youth
    among maidens:
Was it the air? who can say! but in part 'twas
    the charm of the labour.
Still, though a new thing was in me, the poets
    revealed themselves to me,
And in my dreams by Miranda, her Ferdinand,
    often I wandered,
Though all the fuss about girls, the giggling and
    toying and coying,
Were not so strange as before, so incomprehensible
    purely;
Still, as before (and as now), balls, dances, and
    evening parties,
Shooting with bows, going shopping together, and
    hearing them singing,
Dangling beside them, and turning the leaves on
    the dreary piano,
Offering unneeded arms, performing dull farces
    .of escort,
Seemed like a sort of unnatural up-in-the-air
    balloon-work
(Or what to me is as hateful, a riding about in a
    carriage),

C

Utter removal from work, mother earth, and the
    objects of living.
Hungry and fainting for food, you ask me to join
    you in snapping—
What but a pink-paper comfit, with motto romantic
    inside it ?
Wishing to stock me a garden, I'm sent to a table
    of nosegays ;
Better a crust of black bread than a mountain of
    paper confections,
Better a daisy in earth than a dahlia cut and
    gathered,
Better a cowslip with root than a prize carnation
    without it.
    That I allow, said Adam.
              But he, with the bit in his teeth, scarce
Breathed a brief moment, and hurried exultingly
    on with his rider,
Far over hillock, and runnel, and bramble, away
    in the champaign,
Snorting defiance and force, the white foam fleck-
    ing his flanks, the
Rein hanging loose to his neck, and head project-
    ing before him.

    Oh, if they knew and considered, unhappy ones !
    oh, could they see, could
But for a moment discern, how the blood of true
    gallantry kindles,
How the old knightly religion, the chivalry semi-
    quixotic
Stirs in the veins of a man at seeing some delicate
    woman

Serving him, toiling—for him, and the world;
  some tenderest girl, now
Over-weighted, expectant, of him, is it? who shall,
  if only
Duly her burden be lightened, not wholly removed
  from her, mind you,
Lightened if but by the love, the devotion man
  only can offer,
Grand on her pedestal rise as urn-bearing statue
  of Hellas;—
Oh, could they feel at such moments how man's
  heart, as into Eden
Carried anew, seems to see, like the gardener of
  earth uncorrupted,
Eve from the hand of her Maker advancing, an
  help meet for him,
Eve from his own flesh taken, a spirit restored to
  his spirit,
Spirit but not spirit only, himself whatever himself is,
Unto the mystery's end sole helpmate meet to be
  with him;—
Oh, if they saw it and knew it; we soon should
  see them abandon
Boudoir, toilette, carriage, drawing-room, and ball-
  room,
Satin for worsted exchange, gros-de-naples for
  plain linsey-woolsey,
Sandals of silk for clogs, for health lackadaisical
  fancies!
So, feel women, not dolls; so feel the sap of
  existence

Circulate up through their roots from the far-away
    centre of all things,
Circulate up from the depths to the bud on the
    twig that is topmost !
Yes, we should see them delighted, delighted our-
    selves in the seeing,
Bending with blue cotton gown skirted up over
    striped linsey-woolsey,
Milking the kine in the field, like Rachel, watering
    cattle,
Rachel, when at the well the predestined beheld
    and kissed her,
Or, with pail upon head, like Dora beloved of Alexis,
Comely, with well-poised pail over neck arching
    soft to the shoulders,
Comely in gracefullest act, one arm uplifted to
    stay it,
Home from the river or pump moving stately and
    calm to the laundry ;
Ay, doing household work, as many sweet girls I
    have looked at,
Needful household work, which some one, after
    all, must do,   .
Needful, graceful therefore, as washing, cooking,
    and scouring,
Or, if you please, with the fork in the garden
    uprooting potatoes.—
    Or,—high-kilted perhaps, cried Lindsay, at last
    successful,
Lindsay this long time swelling with scorn and
    pent-up fury,
Or high-kilted perhaps, as once at Dundee I saw
    them,

Petticoats up to the knees, or even, it might be,
    above them,
Matching their lily-white legs with the clothes
    that they trod in the wash-tub !
    Laughter ensued at this ; and seeing the Tutor
      embarrassed,
It was from them, I suppose, said Arthur, smiling
    sedately,
Lindsay learnt the tune we all have learnt from
    Lindsay,
For oh, he was a roguey, the Piper o' Dundee.
    Laughter ensued again ; and the Tutor, recover-
      ing slowly,
Said, Are not these perhaps as doubtful as other
    attractions ?
There is a truth in your view, but I think extremely
    distorted ;
Still there is a truth, I own, I understand you
    entirely.
    While the Tutor was gathering his purposes,
      Arthur continued,
Is not all this the same that one hears at common-
    room breakfasts,
Or perhaps Trinity wines, about Gothic buildings
    and Beauty ?
    And with a start from the sofa came Hobbes ;
      with a cry from the sofa,
Where he was laid, the great Hobbes, contempla-
    tive, corpulent, witty,
Author forgotten and silent of currentest phrases
    and fancies,
Mute and exuberant by turns, a fountain at in-
    tervals playing,

Mute and abstracted, or strong and abundant as
    rain in the tropics ;
Studious ; careless of dress ; inobservant : by
    smooth persuasions
Lately decoyed into kilt on example of Hope and
    the Piper,
Hope an Antinoüs mere, Hyperion of calves the
    Piper.
  Beautiful ! cried he up-leaping, analogy perfect
    to madness !
O inexhaustible source of thought, shall I call it,
    or fancy !
Wonderful spring, at whose touch doors fly, what
    a vista disclosing !
Exquisite germ ; Ah no, crude fingers shall not
    soil thee ;
Rest, lovely pearl, in my brain, and slowly mature
    in the oyster.
  While at the exquisite pearl they were laughing
    and corpulent oyster,
Ah, could they only be taught, he resumed, by a
    Pugin of women,
How even churning and washing, the dairy, the
    scullery duties,
Wait but a touch to redeem and convert them to
    charms and attractions,
Scrubbing requires for true grace but frank and
    artistical handling,
And the removal of slops to be ornamentally
    treated.
  Philip who speaks like a book (retiring and
    pausing he added),

Philip, here, who speaks—like a folio say'st thou,
    Piper?
Philip shall write us a book, a Treatise upon *The
    Laws of*
Architectural Beauty in Application to Women;
Illustrations, of course, and a Parker's Glossary
    pendent,
Where shall in specimen seen be the sculliony
    stumpy-columnar
(Which to a reverent taste is perhaps the most
    moving of any),
Rising to grace of true woman in English the
    Early and Later,
Charming us still in fulfilling the Richer and
    Loftier stages,
Lost, ere we end, in the Lady-Debased and the
    Lady-Flamboyant:
Whence why in satire and spite too merciless
    onward pursue her
Hither to hideous close, Modern-Florid, modern-
    fine-lady?
No, I will leave it to you, my Philip, my Pugin of
    women.
    Leave it to Arthur, said Adam, to think of, and
        not to play with.
You are young, you know, he said, resuming, to
    Philip,
You are young, he proceeded, with something of
    fervour to Hewson.
You are a boy; when you grow to a man you'll
    find things alter.
You will then seek only the good, will scorn the
    attractive,

Scorn all mere cosmetics, as now of rank and
    fashion,
Delicate hands, and wealth, so then of poverty
    also,
Poverty truly attractive, more truly, I bear you
    witness.
Good, wherever it's found, you will choose, be it
    humble or stately,
Happy if only you find, and finding do not lose it.
Yes, we must seek what is good, it always and it
    only ;
Not indeed absolute good, good for us, as is said
    in the Ethics,
That which is good for ourselves, our proper
    selves, our best selves.
Ah, you have much to learn, we can't know all
    things at twenty.
Partly you rest on truth, old truth, the duty of
    Duty,
Partly on error, you long for equality.
                       Ay, cried the Piper,
That's what it is, that confounded *égalité*, French
    manufacture,
He is the same as the Chartist who spoke at a
    meeting in Ireland,
What, and is not one man, fellow-men, as good as
    another ?
Faith, replied Pat, *and a deal better too !*
                    So rattled the Piper :
But undisturbed in his tenor, the Tutor.
                       Partly in error
Seeking equality, *is not one woman as good as*
    another ?

I with the Irishman answer, *Yes, better too;* the poorer
Better full oft than richer, than loftier better the lower,
Irrespective of wealth and of poverty, pain and enjoyment,
Women all have their duties, the one as well as the other ;
Are all duties alike ?   Do all alike fulfil them ?
However noble the dream of equality, mark you, Philip,
Nowhere equality reigns in all the world of creation,
Star is not equal to star, nor blossom the same as blossom ;
Herb is not equal to herb, any more than planet to planet.
There is a glory of daisies, a glory again of carnations ;
Were the carnation wise, in gay parterre by greenhouse,
Should it decline to accept the nurture the gardener gives it,
Should it refuse to expand to sun and genial summer,
Simply because the field-daisy that grows in the grass-plat beside it,
Cannot, for some cause or other, develop and be a carnation ?
Would not the daisy itself petition its scrupulous neighbour ?
Up, grow, bloom, and forget me ; be beautiful even to proudness,

E'en for the sake of myself and other poor daisies
  like me.
Education and manners, accomplishments and re-
  finements,
Waltz, peradventure, and polka, the knowledge of
  music and drawing,
All these things are Nature's, to Nature dear and
  precious,
We have all something to do, man, woman alike,
  I own it;
We all have something to do, and in my judgment
  should do it
In our station; not thinking about it, but not
  disregarding;
Holding it, not for enjoyment, but simply because
  we are in it.
  Ah! replied Philip, Alas! the noted phrase of
  the Prayer-book,
*Doing our duty in that state of life to which God
  has called us,*
Seems to me always to mean, when the little rich
  boys say it,
Standing in velvet frock by mamma's brocaded
  flounces,
Eyeing her gold-fastened book and the watch and
  chain at her bosom,
Seems to me always to mean, Eat, drink, and
  never mind others.
  Nay, replied Adam, smiling, so far your economy
  leads me,
Velvet and gold and brocade are nowise to my
  fancy.
Nay, he added, believe me, I like luxurious living

Even as little as you, and grieve in my soul not
    seldom,
More for the rich indeed than the poor, who are
    not so guilty.
  So the discussion closed ; and, said Arthur,
    Now it is my turn,
How will my argument please you ? To-morrow
    we start on our travel.
  And took up Hope the chorus,
            To-morrow we start on our travel.
Lo, the weather is golden, the weather-glass, say
    they, rising ;
Four weeks here have we read ; four weeks will
    we read hereafter ;
Three weeks hence will return and think of classes
    and classics.
Fare ye well, meantime, forgotten, unnamed, un-
    dreamt of,
History, Science, and Poets ! lo, deep in dustiest
    cupboard,
Thookydid, Oloros' son, Halimoosian, here lieth
    buried !
Slumber in Liddell-and-Scott, O musical chaff of
    old Athens,
Dishes, and fishes, bird, beast, and sesquipedalian
    blackguard !
Sleep, weary ghosts, be at peace and abide in
    your lexicon-limbo !
Sleep, as in lava for ages your Herculanean
    kindred,
Sleep, for aught that I care, ' the sleep that knows
    no waking,'

Æschylus, Sophocles, Homer, Herodotus, Pindar,
and Plato.
Three weeks hence be it time to exhume our
dreary classics.
And in the chorus joined Lindsay, the Piper,
the Dialectician,
Three weeks hence we return to the *shop* and
the *wash-hand-stand-basin*
(These are the Piper's names for the bathing-place
and the cottage),
Three weeks hence unbury *Thicksides* and *hairy*
Aldrich.
But the Tutor inquired, the grave man, nick-named
Adam,
Who are they that go, and when do they promise
returning ?
And a silence ensued, and the Tutor himself
continued,
Airlie remains, I presume, he continued, and
Hobbes and Hewson.
Answer was made him by Philip, the poet, the
eloquent speaker :
Airlie remains, I presume, was the answer, and
Hobbes, peradventure ;
Tarry let Airlie May-fairly, and Hobbes, brief-
kilted hero,
Tarry let Hobbes in kilt, and Airlie 'abide in his
breeches ;'
Tarry let these, and read, four Pindars apiece an'
it like them !
Weary of reading am I, and weary of walks pre-
scribed us ;

Weary of Ethic and Logic, of Rhetoric yet more
    weary,
Eager to range over heather unfettered of gillie
    and marquis,
I will away with the rest, and bury my dismal
    classics.
    And to the Tutor rejoining, Be mindful ; you go
       up at Easter,
This was the answer returned by Philip, the Pugin
    of women.
Good are the Ethics I wis ; good absolute, not for
    me, though ;
Good, too, Logic, of course ; in itself, but not in
    fine weather.
Three weeks hence, with the rain, to Prudence,
    Temperance, Justice,
Virtues Moral and Mental, with Latin prose
    included ;
Three weeks hence we return to cares of classes
    and classics.
I will away with the rest, and bury my dismal
    classics.
    But the Tutor inquired, the grave man, nick-
    named Adam,
Where do you mean to go, and whom do you
    mean to visit ?
    And he was answered by Hope, the Viscount,
    His Honour, of Ilay.
Kitcat, a Trinity *coach*, has a party at Drumna-
    drochet,
Up on the side of Loch Ness, in the beautiful
    valley of Urquhart ;

Mainwaring says they will lodge us, and feed us,
    and give us a lift too :
Only they talk ere long to remove to Glenmorison.
    Then at
Castleton, high in Braemar, strange home, with
    his earliest party,
Harrison, fresh from the schools, has James and
    Jones and Lauder.
Thirdly, a Cambridge man I know, Smith, a senior
    wrangler,
With a mathematical score hangs-out at Inveraray.
    Finally, too, from the kilt and the sofa said
    Hobbes in conclusion,
Finally, Philip must hunt for that home of the
    probable poacher,
Hid in the braes of Lochaber, the Bothie of
    What-did-he-call-it.
Hopeless of you and of us, of gillies and marquises
    hopeless,
Weary of Ethic and Logic, of Rhetoric yet more
    weary,
There shall he, smit by the charm of a lovely
    potato-uprooter,
Study the question of sex in the Bothie of *What-
    did-he-call-it.*

III

Namque canebat uti——

So in the golden morning they parted and went
    to the westward.
And in the cottage with Airlie and Hobbes re-
    mained the Tutor ;

Reading nine hours a day with the Tutor, Hobbes
    and Airlie ;
One between bathing and breakfast, and six before
    it was dinner
(Breakfast at eight, at four, after bathing again,
    the dinner),
Finally, two after walking and tea, from nine to
    eleven.
Airlie and Adam at evening their quiet stroll
    together
Took on the terrace-road, with the western hills
    before them ;
Hobbes, only rarely a third, now and then in the
    cottage remaining,
E'en after dinner, eupeptic, would rush yet again
    to his reading ;
Other times, stung by the œstrum of some swift-
    working conception,
Ranged, tearing on in his fury, an Io-cow through
    the mountains,
Heedless of scenery, heedless of bogs, and of
    perspiration,
On the high peaks, unwitting, the hares and
    ptarmigan starting.
    And· the three weeks past, the three weeks,
    three days over,
Neither letter had come, nor casual tidings any,
And the pupils grumbled, the Tutor became
    uneasy,
And in the golden weather they wondered, and
    watched to the westward.
    There is a stream (I name not its name, lest
    inquisitive tourist

Hunt it, and make it a lion, and get it at last into
    guide-books),
Springing far off from a loch unexplored in the
    folds of great mountains,
Falling two miles through rowan and stunted
    alder, enveloped
Then for four more in a forest of pine, where
    broad and ample
Spreads, to convey it, the glen with heathery
    slopes on both sides :
Broad and fair the stream, with occasional falls
    and narrows ;
But, where the glen of its course approaches the
    vale of the river,
Met and blocked by a huge interposing mass of
    granite,
Scarce by a channel deep-cut, raging up, and
    raging onward,
Forces its flood through a passage so narrow a
    lady would step it.
There, across the great rocky wharves, a wooden
    bridge goes,
Carrying a path to the forest ; below, three
    hundred yards, say,
Lower in level some twenty-five feet, through flats
    of shingle,
Stepping-stones and a cart-track cross in the open
    valley.
    But in the interval here the boiling pent-up
      water
Frees itself by a final descent, attaining a basin,
Ten feet wide and eighteen long, with whiteness
    and fury

Occupied partly, but mostly pellucid, pure, a
    mirror ;
Beautiful there for the colour derived from green
    rocks under ;
Beautiful, most of all, where beads of foam up-
    rising
Mingle their clouds of white with the delicate
    hue of the stillness,
Cliff over cliff for its sides, with rowan and pendent
    birch boughs,
Here it lies, unthought of above at the bridge
    and pathway,
Still more enclosed from below by wood and
    rocky projection.
You are shut in, left alone with yourself and per-
    fection of water,
Hid on all sides, left alone with yourself and the
    goddess of bathing.
  Here, the pride of the plunger, you stride the
   ·   fall and clear it ;
Here, the delight of the bather, you roll in beaded
    sparklings,
Here into pure green depth drop down from lofty
    ledges.
  Hither, a month agone, they had come, and
    discovered it ; hither
(Long a design, but long unaccountably left un-
    accomplished),
Leaving the well-known bridge and pathway above
    to the forest,
Turning below from the track of the carts over
    stone and shingle,

Piercing a wood, and skirting a narrow and natural
causeway
Under the rocky wall that hedges the bed of the
streamlet,   .
Rounded a craggy point, and saw on a sudden
before them
Slabs of rock, and a tiny beach, and perfection of
water,
Picture-like beauty, seclusion sublime, and the
goddess of bathing.
There they bathed, of course, and Arthur, the Glory
of headers,
Leapt from the ledges with Hope, he twenty feet,
he thirty;
There, overbold, great Hobbes from a ten-foot
height descended,
Prone, as a quadruped, prone with hands and feet
protending;
There in the sparkling champagne, ecstatic, they
shrieked and shouted.
'Hobbes's gutter' the Piper entitles the spot,
profanely,
Hope 'the Glory' would have, after Arthur, the
Glory of headers:
But, for before they departed, in shy and fugitive
reflex,
Here in the eddies and there did the splendour of
Jupiter glimmer;
Adam adjudged it the name of Hesperus, star of
the evening.
Hither, to Hesperus, now, the star of evening
above them,

Come in their lonelier walk the pupils twain and
    Tutor ;
Turned from the track of the carts, and passing
    the stone and shingle,
Piercing the wood, and skirting the stream by the
    natural causeway,
Rounded the craggy point, and now at their ease
    looked up ; and
Lo, on the rocky ledge, regardant, the Glory of
    headers,
Lo, on the beach, expecting the plunge, not cigar-
    less, the Piper,—
    And they looked, and wondered, incredulous,
      looking yet once more.
Yes, it was he, on the ledge, bare-limbed, an Apollo,
    down-gazing,
Eyeing one moment the beauty, the life, ere he
    flung himself in it,
Eyeing through eddying green waters the green-
    tinting floor underneath them,
Eyeing the bead on the surface, the bead, like a
    cloud rising to it,
Drinking-in, deep in his soul, the beautiful hue
    and the clearness,
Arthur, the shapely, the brave, the unboasting, the
    Glory of headers ;
Yes, and with fragrant weed, by his knapsack,
    spectator and critic,
Seated on slab by the margin, the Piper, the Cloud-
    compeller.
    Yes, they were come ; were restored to the party,
      its grace and its gladness,

Yes, were here, as of old ; the light-giving orb of
    the household,
Arthur, the shapely, the tranquil, the strength-and-
    contentment diffusing,
In the pure presence of whom none could quarrel
    long, nor be pettish,
And, the gay fountain of mirth, their dearly beloved
    of Pipers ;
Yes, they were come, were here : but Hewson and
    Hope—where they then ?
Are they behind, travel-sore, or ahead, going
    straight, by the pathway ?
    And from his seat and cigar spoke the Piper,
    the Cloud-compeller.
Hope with the uncle abideth for shooting.   Ah
    me, were I with him !
Ah, good boy that I am, to have stuck to my word
    and my reading !
Good, good boy to be here, far away, who might
    be at Balloch !
Only one day to have stayed who might have been
    welcome for seven,
Seven whole days in castle and forest—gay in the
    mazy
Moving, imbibing the rosy, and pointing a gun at
    the horny !
    And the Tutor impatient, expectant, interrupted.
Hope with the uncle, and Hewson—with him ? or
    where have you left him ?
    And from his seat and cigar spoke the Piper, the
    Cloud-compeller.
Hope with the uncle, and Hewson—Why, Hewson
    we left in Rannoch,

By the lochside and the pines, in a farmer's house,
    —reflecting—
Helping to shear,[1] and dry clothes, and bring in
    peat from the peat-stack.
  And the Tutor's countenance fell ; perplexed,
    dumb-foundered
Stood he,—slow and with pain disengaging jest
    from earnest.
  He is not far from home, said Arthur from the
    water,
He will be with us to-morrow, at latest, or the
    next day,
  And he was even more reassured by the Piper's
    rejoinder.
Can he have come by the mail, and have got to
    the cottage before us ?
  So to the cottage they went, and Philip was
    not at the cottage ;
But by the mail was a letter from Hope, who
    himself was to follow.
  Two whole days and nights succeeding brought
    not Philip,
Two whole days and nights exhausted not question
    and story.
  For it was told, the Piper narrating, corrected
    of Arthur.
Often by word corrected, more often by smile and
    motion,
How they had been to Iona, to Staffa, to Skye, to
    Culloden,
Seen Loch Awe, Loch Tay, Loch Fyne, Loch
    Ness, Loch Arkaig,

[1] Reap.

Been up Ben-nevis, Ben-more, Ben-cruachan, Ben-
    muick-dhui ;
How they had walked, and eaten, and drunken,
    and slept in kitchens,
Slept upon floors of kitchens, and tasted the real
    Glenlivat,
Walked up perpendicular hills, and also down
    them,
Hither and thither had been, and this and that
    had witnessed,
Left not a thing to be done, and had not a copper
    remaining.
    For it was told withal, he telling, and he
    correcting,
How in the race they had run, and beaten the
    gillies of Rannoch,
How in forbidden glens, in Mar and midmost Athol,
Philip insisting hotly, and Arthur and Hope
    compliant,
They had defied the keepers ; the Piper alone
    protesting,
Liking the fun, it was plain, in his heart, but
    tender of game-law ;
Yea, too, in Meäly glen, the heart of Lochiel's
    fair forest,
Where Scotch firs are darkest and amplest, and
    intermingle
Grandly with rowan and ash—in Mar you have
    no ashes,
There the pine is alone, or relieved by the birch
    and the alder—
How in Meäly glen, while stags were starting
    before, they

Made the watcher believe they were guests from
 Achnacarry.
 And there was told moreover, he telling, the
 other correcting,
Often by word, more often by mute significant
 motion,
Much of the Cambridge *coach* and his pupils at
 Inveraray,
Huge barbarian pupils, Expanded in Infinite
 Series,
Firing-off signal guns (great scandal) from window
 to window
(For they were lodging perforce in distant and
 numerous houses),
Signals, when, one retiring, another should go to
 the Tutor :—
Much too of Kitcat, of course, and the party at
 Drumnadrochet,
Mainwaring, Foley, and Fraser, their idleness
 horrid and dog-cart ;
Drumnadrochet was *seedy*, Glenmorison *adequate*,
 but at
Castleton, high in Braemar, were the *clippingest*
 places for bathing ;
One by the bridge in the village, indecent, the
 Town Hall christened,
Where had Lauder howbeit been bathing, and
 Harrison also,
Harrison even, the Tutor ; another like Hesperus
 here, and
Up the water of Eye, half-a-dozen at least, all
 stunners.

And it was told, the Piper narrating and Arthur
  correcting,
Colouring he, dilating, magniloquent, glorying in
  picture,
He to a matter-of-fact still softening, paring,
  abating,
He to the great might-have-been upsoaring, sublime
  and ideal,
He to the merest it-was restricting, diminishing,
  dwarfing,
River to streamlet reducing, and fall to slope
  subduing :
So was it told, the Piper narrating, corrected of
  Arthur,
How under Linn of Dee, where over rocks,
  between rocks,
Freed from prison the river comes, pouring, rolling,
  rushing,
Then at a sudden descent goes sliding, gliding,
  unbroken,
Falling, sliding, gliding, in narrow space collected,
Save for a ripple at last, a sheeted descent un-
  broken,—
How to the element offering their bodies, down-
  shooting the fall, they
Mingled themselves with the flood and the force
  of imperious water.
  And it was told too, Arthur narrating, the
    Piper correcting,
How, as one comes to the level, the weight of the
  downward impulse
Carries the head under water, delightful, unspeak-
  able ; how the

Piper, here ducked and blinded, got stray, and
  borne-off by the current
Wounded his lily-white thighs, below, at the
  craggy corner.
  And it was told, the Piper resuming, corrected
  of Arthur,
More by word than motion, change ominous,
  noted of Adam,
How at the floating-bridge of Laggan, one morn-
  ing at sunrise,
Came, in default of the ferryman, out of her bed
  a brave lassie ;
And as Philip and she together were turning the
  handles,
Winding the chain by which the boat works over
  the water,
Hands intermingled with hands, and at last, as
  they stepped from the boatie,
Turning about, they saw lips also mingle with lips ;
  but
That was flatly denied and loudly exclaimed at by
  Arthur :
How at the General's hut, the Inn by the Foyers
  Fall, where
Over the loch looks at you the summit of Méal-
  fourvónie,
How here too he was hunted at morning, and
  found in the kitchen
Watching the porridge being made, pronouncing
  them smoked for certain,
Watching the porridge being made, and asking
  the lassie that made them

What was the Gaelic for *girl*, and what was the
    Gaelic for *pretty;*
How in confusion he shouldered his knapsack, yet
    blushingly stammered,
Waving a hand to the lassie, that blushingly bent
    o'er the porridge,
Something outlandish—*Slan*-something, *Slan leat,*
    he believed, *Caleg Looach*—
That was the Gaelic, it seemed, for 'I bid you
    good-bye, bonnie lassie ;'
Arthur admitted it true, not of Philip, but of the
    Piper.
    And it was told by the Piper, while Arthur
    looked out at the window,
How in thunder and in rain—it is wetter far to
    the westward—
Thunder and rain and wind, losing heart and
    road, they were welcomed,
Welcomed, and three days detained at a farm by
    the lochside of Rannoch ;
How in the three days' detention was Philip ob-
    served to be smitten,
Smitten by golden-haired Katie, the youngest and
    comeliest daughter ;
Was he not seen, even Arthur observed it, from
    breakfast to bedtime,
Following her motions with eyes ever brightening,
    softening ever ?
Did he not fume, fret, and fidget to find her stand
    waiting at table ?
Was he not one mere St. Vitus' dance, when he
    saw her at nightfall

Go through the rain to fetch peat, through beating
rain to the peat-stack?
How too a dance, as it happened, was given by
Grant of Glenurchie,
And with the farmer they went as the farmer's
guests to attend it;
Philip stayed dancing till daylight,—and evermore
with Katie;
How the whole next afternoon he was with her
away in the shearing,[1]
And the next morning ensuing was found in the
ingle beside her
Kneeling, picking the peats from her apron,—
blowing together,
Both, between laughing, with lips distended, to
kindle the embers;
Lips were so near to lips, one living cheek to
another,—
Though, it was true, he was shy, very shy,—yet
it wasn't in nature,
Wasn't in nature, the Piper averred, there shouldn't
be kissing;
So when at noon they had packed up the things,
and proposed to be starting,
Philip professed he was lame, would leave in the
morning and follow;
Follow he did not; do burns, when you go up a
glen, follow after?
Follow, he had not, nor left; do needles leave the
loadstone?
Nay, they had turned after starting, and looked
through the trees at the corner,

[1] Reaping.

Lo, on the rocks by the lake there he was, the
    lassie beside him,
Lo, there he was, stooping by her, and helping
    with stones from the water
Safe in the wind to keep down the clothes she
    would spread for the drying.
There they had left him, and there, if Katie was
    there, was Philip,
There drying clothes, making fires, making love,
    getting on too by this time,
Though he was shy, so exceedingly shy.
                 You may say so, said Arthur,
For the first time they had known with a peevish
    intonation,—
Did not the Piper himself flirt more in a single
    evening,
Namely, with Janet the elder, than Philip in all
    our sojourn ?
Philip had stayed, it was true ; the Piper was
    loth to depart too,
Harder his parting from Janet than e'en from the
    keeper at Balloch ;
And it was certain that Philip was lame.
                 Yes, in his excuses,
Answered the Piper, indeed !—
            But tell me, said Hobbes interposing,
Did you not say she was seen every day in her
    beauty and bedgown
Doing plain household work, as washing, cooking,
    scouring ?
How could he help but love her ? nor lacked there
    perhaps the attraction

That, in a blue cotton print tucked up over striped
    linsey-woolsey,
Barefoot, barelegged, he beheld her, with arms
    bare up to the elbows,
Bending with fork in her hand in a garden up-
    rooting potatoes?
Is not Katie as Rachel, and is not Philip a Jacob?
Truly Jacob, supplanting a hairy Highland Esau?
Shall he not, love-entertained, feed sheep for the
    Laban of Rannoch?
Patriarch happier he, the long servitude ended of
    wooing,
If when he wake in the morning he find not a
    Leah beside him!
  But the Tutor inquired, who had bit his lip to
    bleeding,
How far off is the place? who will guide me
    thither to-morrow?

  But by the mail, ere the morrow, came Hope,
    and brought new tidings;
Round by Rannoch had come, and Philip was not
    at Rannoch;
He had left at noon, an hour ago.
                        With the lassie?
With her? the Piper exclaimed.   Undoubtedly!
    By great Jingo!
And upon that he arose, slapping both his thighs
    like a hero,
Partly for emphasis only, to mark his conviction,
    but also
Part in delight at the fun, and the joy of eventful
    living.

Hope couldn't tell him, of course, but thought
    it improbable wholly ;
Janet, the Piper's friend, he had seen, and she
    didn't say so,
Though she asked a good deal about Philip, and
    where he was gone to :
One odd thing, by the bye, he continued, befell
    me while with her ;
Standing beside her, I saw a girl pass ; I thought
    I had seen her,
Somewhat remarkable-looking, elsewhere ; and
    asked what her name was ;
Elspie Mackaye, was the answer, the daughter of
    David ! she's stopping
Just above here, with her uncle. And David
    Mackaye, where lives he ?
It's away west, she said ; they call it Tober-na-
    vuolich.

IV

Ut vidi, ut perii, ut me malus abstulit error

So in the golden weather they waited. But
    Philip returned not.
Sunday six days thence a letter arrived in his
    writing.—
But, O Muse, that encompassest Earth like the
    ambient ether,
Swifter than steamer or railway or magical missive
    electric,
Belting like Ariel the sphere with the star-like
    trail of thy travel,

Thou with thy Poet, to mortals mere post-office
    second-hand knowledge
Leaving, wilt seek in the moorland of Rannoch
    the wandering hero.
  There is it, there, or in lofty Lochaber, where,
    silent upheaving,
Heaving from ocean to sky, and under snow-winds
    of September,
Visibly whitening at morn to darken by noon in
    the shining,
Rise on their mighty foundations the brethren
    huge of Ben-nevis?
There, or westward away, where roads are un-
    known to Loch Nevish,
And the great peaks look abroad over Skye to the
    westernmost islands?
There is it? there? or there? we shall find our
    wandering hero?
  Here, in Badenoch, here, in Lochaber anon, in
    Lochiel, in
Knoydart, Moydart, Morrer, Ardgower, and Ard-
    namurchan,
Here I see him and here: I see him; anon I lose
    him!
Even as cloud passing subtly unseen from moun-
    tain to mountain,
Leaving the crest of Ben-more to be palpable next
    on Ben-vohrlich,
Or like to hawk of the hill which ranges and soars
    in its hunting,
Seen and unseen by turns, now here, now in ether
    eludent.

Wherefore, as cloud of Ben-more or hawk
    over-ranging the mountains,
Wherefore in Badenoch drear, in lofty Lochaber,
    Lochiel, and
Knoydart, Moydart, Morrer, Ardgower, and Ard-
    namurchan,
Wandereth he who should either with Adam be
    studying logic,
Or by the lochside of Rannoch on Katie his
    rhetoric úsing ;
He who, his three weeks past, past now long ago,
    to the cottage
Punctual promised return to cares of classes and
    classics,
He who, smit to the heart by that youngest
    comeliest daughter,
Bent, unregardful of spies, at her feet, spreading
    clothes from her wash-tub ?
Can it be with him through Badenoch, Morrer,
    and Ardnamurchan ;
Can it be with him he beareth the golden-haired
    lassie of Rannoch ?
This fierce, furious walking—o'er mountain-top
    and moorland,
Sleeping in shieling and bothie, with drover on
    hill-side sleeping,
Folded in plaid, where sheep are strewn thicker
    than rocks by Loch Awen,
This fierce, furious travel unwearying—cannot in
    truth be
Merely the wedding tour succeeding the week of
    wooing !

No, wherever be Katie, with Philip she is not;
    I see him,
Lo, and he sitteth alone, and these are his words
    in the mountain.
    Spirits escaped from the body can enter and be
    with the living;
Entering unseen, and retiring unquestioned, they
    bring,—do they feel too?—
Joy, pure joy, as they mingle and mix inner
    essence with essence;
Would I were dead, I keep saying, that so I
    could go and uphold her!
Joy, pure joy, bringing with them, and, when they
    retire, leaving after
No cruel shame, no prostration, despondency;
    memories rather,
Sweet happy hopes bequeathing. Ah! wherefore
    not thus with the living?
Would I were dead, I keep saying, that so I
    could go and uphold her!
    Is it impossible, say you, these passionate
    fervent impulsions,
These projections of spirit to spirit, these inward
    embraces,
Should in strange ways, in her dreams, should
    visit her, strengthen her, shield her?
Is it possible, rather, that these great floods of
    feeling
Setting-in daily from me towards her should,
    impotent wholly,
Bring neither sound nor motion to that sweet
    shore they heave to?
Efflux here, and there no stir nor pulse of influx!

Would I were dead, I keep saying, that so I
 could go and uphold her!
Surely, surely, when sleepless I lie in the mountain
 lamenting,
Surely, surely, she hears in her dreams a voice, 'I
 am with thee,'
Saying, 'although not with thee; behold, for we
 mated our spirits
Then, when we stood in the chamber, and knew
 not the words we were saying;'
Yea, if she felt me within her, when not with one
 finger I touched her,
Surely she knows it, and feels it while sorrowing
 here in the moorland.
Would I were dead, I keep saying, that so I
 could go and uphold her!
 Spirits with spirits commingle and separate;
  lightly as winds do,
Spice-laden South with the ocean-born zephyr!
 they mingle and sunder;
No sad remorses for them, no visions of horror
 and vileness.
Would I were dead, I keep saying, that so I
 could go and uphold her!
 Surely the force that here sweeps me along in
  its violent impulse,
Surely my strength shall be in her, my help and
 protection about her,
Surely in inner-sweet gladness and vigour of joy
 shall sustain her,
Till, the brief winter o'er-past, her own true sap in
 the springtide

Rise, and the tree I have bared be verdurous e'en
    as aforetime !
Surely it may be, it should be, it must be.   Yet
    ever and ever,
Would I were dead, I keep saying, that so I
    could go and uphold her !
   No, wherever be Katie, with Philip she is not :
       behold, for
Here he is sitting alone, and these are his words
    in the mountain.
   And, at the farm on the lochside of Rannoch, in
       parlour and kitchen,
Hark ! there is music—the flowing of music, of
    milk, and of whisky ;
Lo, I see piping and dancing ! and whom in the
    midst of the battle
Cantering loudly along there, or, look you, with
    arms uplifted,
Whistling, and snapping his fingers, and seizing
    his gay-smiling Janet,
Whom ?—whom else but the Piper ? the wary
    precognisant Piper,
Who, for the love of gay Janet, and mindful of old
    invitation,
Putting it quite as a duty and urging grave claims
    to attention,
True to his night had crossed over : there goeth
    he, brimful of music,
Like a cork tossed by the eddies that foam under
    furious lasher,
Like to skiff, lifted, uplifted, in lock, by the swift-
    swelling sluices,

So with the music possessing him, swaying him,
  goeth he, look you,
Swinging and flinging, and stamping and tramp-
  ing, and grasping and clasping
Whom but gay Janet?—Him rivalling, Hobbes,
  briefest-kilted of heroes,
Enters, O stoutest, O rashest of creatures, mere
  fool of a Saxon,
Skill-less of philabeg, skill-less of reel too,—the
  whirl and the twirl o't:
Him see I frisking, and whisking, and ever at
  swifter gyration
Under brief curtain revealing broad acres—not of
  broad cloth.
Him see I there and the Piper—the Piper what
  vision beholds not?
Him and His Honour with Arthur, with Janet our
  Piper, and is it,
Is it, O marvel of marvels! he too in the maze of
  the mazy,
Skipping, and tripping, though stately, though
  languid, with head on one shoulder,
Airlie, with sight of the waistcoat the golden-
  haired Katie consoling?
Katie, who simple and comely, and smiling and
  blushing as ever,
What though she wear on that neck a blue kerchief
  remembered as Philip's,
Seems in her maidenly freedom to need small
  consolement of waistcoats!—
  Wherefore in Badenoch then, far-away, in
  Lochaber, Lochiel, in

Knoydart, Moydart, Morrer, Ardgower, or Ardna-
  murchan,
Wanders o'er mountain and moorland, in shieling
  or bothic is sleeping,
He, who,—and why should he not then ? capri-
  cious ? or is it rejected ?
Might to the piping of Rannoch be pressing the
  thrilling fair fingers,
Might, as he clasped her, transmit to her bosom
  the throb of his own—yea,—
Might in the joy of the reel be wooing and winning
  his Katie ?
  What is it Adam reads far off by himself in the
  cottage ?
Reads yet again with emotion, again is preparing
  to answer ?
What is it Adam is reading ?   What was it Philip
  had written ?
  There was it writ, how Philip possessed
  undoubtedly had been,
Deeply, entirely possessed by the charm of the
  maiden of Rannoch ;
Deeply as never before ! how sweet and bewitching
  he felt her
Seen still before him at work, in the garden, the
  byre, the kitchen ;
How it was beautiful to him to stoop at her side
  in the shearing,
Binding uncouthly the ears that fell from her
  dexterous sickle,
Building uncouthly the stooks,[1] which she laid by
  her sickle to straighten,

  [1] Shocks.

How at the dance he had broken through shyness ;
   for four days after
Lived on her eyes, unspeaking what lacked not ‑
   articulate speaking ;
Felt too that she too was feeling what he did.—
   Howbeit they parted !
How by a kiss from her lips he had seemed made
   nobler and stronger,
Yea, for the first time in life a man complete and
   perfect,
So forth ! much that before has been heard of.—
   Howbeit they parted !
  What had ended it all, he said, was singular,
   very.—
I was walking along some two miles off from the
   cottage
Full of my dreamings—a girl went by in a party
   with others ;
She had a cloak on, was stepping on quickly, for
   rain was beginning ;
But as she passed, from her hood I saw her eyes
   look at me.
So quick a glance, so regardless I, that although
   I had felt it,
You couldn't properly say our eyes met.   She cast
   ·it, and left it :
It was three minutes perhaps ere I knew what it
   was.   I had seen her
Somewhere before I am sure, but that wasn't it ;
   not its import :
No, it had seemed to regard me with simple
   superior insight,

Quietly saying to itself—Yes, there he is still in
    his fancy,
Letting drop from him at random as things not
    worth his considering
All the benefits gathered and put in his hands by
    fortune,
Loosing a hold which others, contented and
    unambitious,
Trying down here to keep up, know the value of
    better than he does.
What is this? was it perhaps?—Yes, there he is
    still in his fancy,
Doesn't yet see we have here just the things he
    is used to elsewhere ;
People here too are people and not as fairy-land
    creatures ;
He is in a trance, and possessed ; I wonder how
    long to continue ;
It is a shame and a pity—and no good likely to
    follow.—
Something like this, but indeed I cannot attempt
    to define it.
Only, three hours thence I was off and away in
    the moorland,
Hiding myself from myself if I could ; the arrow
    within me.
Katie was not in the house, thank God : I saw her
    in passing,
Saw her, unseen myself, with the pang of a cruel
    desertion ;
What she thinks about it, God knows ! poor child ;
    may she only

Think me a fool and a madman, and no more
    worth her remembering !
Meantime all through the mountains I hurry and
    know not whither,
Tramp along here, and think, and know not what
    I should think.
  Tell me then, why, as I sleep amid hill-tops
    high in the moorland,
Still in my dreams I am pacing the streets of the
    dissolute city,
Where dressy girls slithering by upon pavements
    give sign for accosting,
Paint on their beautiless cheeks, and hunger and
    shame in their bosoms ;
Hunger by drink, and by that which they shudder
    yet burn for, appeasing,—
Hiding their shame—ah God !—in the glare of
    the public gas-lights ?
Why, while I feel my ears catching through
    slumber the run of the streamlet,
Still am I pacing the pavement, and seeing the
    sign for accosting,
Still am I passing those figures, not daring to look
    in their faces ?
Why, when the chill, ere the light, of the daybreak
    uneasily wakes me,
Find I a cry in my heart crying up to the heaven
    of heavens,
No, Great Unjust Judge ! she is purity ; I am the
    lost one.
  You will not think that I soberly look for such
    things for sweet Katie ;

No, but the vision is on me; I now first see how
    it happens,
Feel how tender and soft is the heart of a girl; how passive
Fain would it be, how helpless; and helplessness
    leads to destruction.
Maiden reserve torn from off it, grows never again
    to reclothe it,
Modesty broken through once to immodesty flies
    for protection.
Oh, who saws through the trunk, though he leave
    the tree up in the forest,
When the next wind casts it down,—is *his* not
    the hand that smote it?
    This is the answer, the second, which, pondering
      long with emotion,
There by himself in the cottage the Tutor addressed
    to Philip.
    I have perhaps been severe, dear Philip, and
      hasty; forgive me;
For I was fain to reply ere I wholly had read
    through your letter;
And it was written in scraps with crossings and
    counter-crossings
Hard to connect with each other correctly, and
    hard to decipher;
Paper was scarce, I suppose: forgive me; I write
    to console you.
    Grace is given of God, but knowledge is bought
      in the market;
Knowledge needful for all, yet cannot be had for
    the asking.

There are exceptional beings, one finds them
    distant and rarely,
Who, endowed with the vision alike and the
    interpretation,
See, by the neighbours' eyes and their own still
    motions enlightened,
In the beginning the end, in the acorn the oak of
    the forest,
In the child of to-day its children to long genera-
    tions,
In a thought or a wish a life, a drama, an epos.
There are inheritors, is it ? by mystical genera-
    tion
Heiring the wisdom and ripeness of spirits gone
    by ; without labour
Owning what others by doing and suffering earn ;
    what old men
After long years of mistake and erasure are proud
    to have come to,
Sick with mistake and erasure possess when
    possession is idle.
Yes, there is power upon earth, seen feebly in
    women and children,
Which can, laying one hand on the cover, read
    off, unfaltering,
Leaf after leaf unlifted, the words of the closed
    book under,
Words which we are poring at, hammering at,
    stumbling at, spelling.
Rare is this ; wisdom mostly is bought for a price
    in the market ;—
Rare is this ; and happy, who buys so much for
    so little,

As I conceive have you, and as I will hope has
    Katie.
Knowledge is needful for man,—needful no less
    for woman,
Even in Highland glens, were they vacant of
    shooter and tourist.
Not that, of course, I mean to prefer your blindfold
    hurry
Unto a soul that abides most loving yet most
    withholding ;
Least unfeeling though calm, self-contained yet
    most unselfish ;
Renders help and accepts it, a man among men
    that are brothers,
Views, not plucks the beauty, adores, and demands
    no embracing,
So in its peaceful passage whatever is lovely and
    gracious
Still without seizing or spoiling, itself in itself
    reproducing.
No, I do not set Philip herein on the level of
    Arthur ;
No, I do not compare still tarn with furious torrent,
Yet will the tarn overflow, assuaged in the lake be
    the torrent.
    Women are weak, as you say, and love of all
    things to be passive,
Passive, patient, receptive, yea, even of wrong
    and misdoing,
Even to force and misdoing with joy and victorious
    feeling
Patient, passive, receptive ; for that is the strength
    of their being,

Like to the earth taking all things, and all to
    good converting.
Oh 'tis a snare indeed!—Moreover, remember it,
    Philip,
To the prestige of the richer the lowly are prone
    to be yielding,
Think that in dealing with them they are raised
    to a different region,
Where old laws and morals are modified, lost,
    exist not ;
Ignorant they as they are, they have but to con-
    form and be yielding.
  But I have spoken of this already, and need
    not repeat it.
You will not now run after what merely attracts
    and entices,
Every-day things highly-coloured, and common-
    place carved and gilded.
You will henceforth seek only the good : and seek
    it, Philip,
Where it is—not more abundant, perhaps, but—
    more easily met with ;
Where you are surer to find it, less likely to run
    into error,
In your station, not thinking about it, but not
    disregarding.
  So was the letter completed : a postscript after-
    ward added,   .
Telling the tale that was told by the dancers re-
    turning from Rannoch.
So was the letter completed : but query, whither
    to send it ?

Not for the will of the wisp, the cloud, and the
   hawk of the moorland,
Ranging afar thro' Lochaber, Lochiel, and Knoydart, and Moydart,
Have even latest extensions adjusted a postal
   arrangement.
Query resolved very shortly, when Hope, from
   his chamber descending,
Came with a note in his hand from the Lady, his
   aunt, at the Castle ;
Came and revealed the contents of a missive that
   brought strange tidings ;
Came and announced to the friends, in a voice
   that was husky with wonder,
Philip was staying at Balloch, was there in the
   room with the Countess,
Philip to Balloch had come and was dancing with
   Lady Maria.
   Philip at Balloch, he said, after all that stately
      refusal,
He there at last—O strange ! O marvel, marvel
   of marvels !
Airlie, the Waistcoat, with Katie, we left him this
   morning at Rannoch ;
Airlie with Katie, he said, and Philip with Lady
   Maria.
   And amid laughter Adam paced up and down,
      repeating
Over and over, unconscious, the phrase which
   Hope had lent him,
Dancing at Balloch, you say, in the Castle, with
   Lady Maria.

V

———*Putavi*
Stultus ego huic nostræ similem.

So in the cottage with Adam the pupils five to-
gether
Duly remained, and read, and looked no more for
Philip,
Philip at Balloch shooting and dancing with Lady
Maria.
Breakfast at eight, and now, for brief September
daylight,
Luncheon at two, and dinner at seven, or even
later,
Five full hours between for the loch and the glen
and the mountain,—
So in the joy of their life and glory of shooting-
jackets,
So they read and roamed, the pupils five with
Adam.
 What if autumnal shower came frequent and
chill from the westward,
What if on browner sward with yellow leaves
besprinkled,
Gemming the crispy blade, the delicate gossamer
gemming,
Frequent and thick lay at morning the chilly beads
of hoar-frost,
Duly in *matutine* still, and daily, whatever the
weather,
Bathed in the rain and the frost and the mist with.
the Glory of headers

Hope.   Thither also at times, of cold and of
    possible gutters
Careless, unmindful, unconscious, would Hobbes,
    or ere they departed,
Come, in heavy pea-coat his trouserless trunk
    enfolding,
Come, under coat over-brief those lusty legs dis-
    playing,
All from the shirt to the slipper the natural man
    revealing.
  Duly there they bathed and daily, the twain or
    the trio,
Where in the morning was custom, where over a
    ledge of granite
Into a granite basin the amber torrent descended :
Beautiful, very, to gaze in ere plunging ; beautiful
    also,
Perfect as picture, as vision entrancing that comes
    to the sightless,
Through the great granite jambs the stream, the
    glen, and the mountain,
Beautiful, seen by snatches in intervals of dressing,
Morn after morn, unsought for, recurring ; them-
    selves too seeming
Not as spectators, accepted into it, immingled, as
    truly
Part of it as are the kine in the field lying there
    by the birches.
  So they bathed, they read, they roamed in glen
    and forest ;
Far amid blackest pines to the waterfall they
    shadow,

Far up the long, long glen to the loch, and the
  loch beyond it,
Deep, under huge red cliffs, a secret ; and oft by
  the starlight,
Or the aurora, perchance, racing home for the
  eight o'clock mutton.
So they bathed, and read, and roamed in heathery
  Highland ;
There in the joy of their life and glory of shooting-
  jackets
Bathed and read and roamed, and looked no more
  for Philip.

List to a letter that came from Philip at Balloch
  to Adam.
  I am here, O my friend !—idle, but learning
  wisdom.
Doing penance, you think ; content, if so, in my
  penance.
  Often I find myself saying, while watching in
  dance or on horseback
One that is here, in her freedom and grace, and
  imperial sweetness,
Often I find myself saying, old faith and doctrine
  abjuring,
Into the crucible casting philosophies, facts,
  convictions,—
Were it not well that the stem should be naked of
  leaf and of tendril,
Poverty-stricken, the barest, the dismallest stick
  of the garden ;
Flowerless, leafless, unlovely, for ninety-and-nine
  long summers,

So in the hundredth, at last, were bloom for one
    day at the summit,
So but that fleeting flower were lovely as Lady
    Maria.
  Often I find myself saying, and know not
    myself as I say it,
What of the poor and the weary? their labour
    and pain is needed.
Perish the poor and the weary! what can they
    better than perish,
Perish in labour for her, who is worth the
    destruction of empires?
What! for a mite, for a mote, an impalpable
    odour of honour,
Armies shall bleed; cities burn; and the soldier
    red from the storming
Carry hot rancour and lust into chambers of
    mothers and daughters:
What! would ourselves for the cause of an hour
    encounter the battle,
Slay and be slain; lie rotting in hospital, hulk,
    and prison:
Die as a dog dies; die mistaken perhaps, and
    dishonoured.
Yea,—and shall hodmen in beer-shops complain
    of a glory denied them,
Which could not ever be theirs more than now it
    is theirs as spectators?
Which could not be, in all earth, if it were not
    for labour of hodmen?
  And I find myself saying, and what I am
    saying, discern not,

Dig in thy deep dark prison, O miner ! and finding
    be thankful ;
Though unpolished by thee, unto thee unseen in
    perfection,
While thou art eating black bread in the poisonous
    air of thy cavern,
Far away glitters the gem on the peerless neck of
    a Princess.
Dig, and starve, and be thankful ; it is so, and
    thou hast been aiding.
  Often I find myself saying, in irony is it, or
    earnest ?
Yea, what is more, be rich, O ye rich ! be sublime
    in great houses,
Purple and delicate linen endure ; be of Burgundy
    patient ;
Suffer that service be done you, permit of the page
    and the valet,
Vex not your souls with annoyance of charity
    schools or of districts,
Cast not to swine of the sty the pearls that should
    gleam in your foreheads.
Live, be lovely, forget them, be beautiful even to
    proudness,
Even for their poor sakes whose happiness is to
    behold you ;
Live, be uncaring, be joyous, be sumptuous ; only
    be lovely,—
Sumptuous not for display, and joyous, not for
    enjoyment ;
Not for enjoyment truly ; for Beauty and God's
    great glory !

Yes, and I say, and it seems inspiration—of Good or of Evil !

Is it not He that hath done it, and who shall dare gainsay it ?

Is it not even of Him, who hath made us ?—Yea, *for the lions,*

Roaring after their prey, do seek their meat from God !

Is it not even of Him, who one kind over another

All the works of His hand hath disposed in a wonderful order ?

Who hath made man, as the beasts, to live the one on the other,

Who hath made man as Himself to know the law · —and accept it !

You will wonder at this, no doubt ! I also wonder !

But we must live and learn ; we can't know all things at twenty.

List to a letter of Hobbes to Philip his friend at Balloch.

All Cathedrals are Christian, all Christians are Cathedrals,

Such is the Catholic doctrine ; 'tis ours with a slight variation ;

Every woman is, or ought to be, a Cathedral,

Built on the ancient plan, a Cathedral pure and perfect,

Built by that only law, that Use be suggester of Beauty,

Nothing concealed that is done, but all things done to adornment,

Meanest utilities seized as occasions to grace and
    embellish.—
  So had I duly commenced in the spirit and
    style of my Philip,
So had I formally opened the Treatise upon *the
    Laws of*
Architectural Beauty in Application to Women,
So had I writ.—But my fancies are palsied by
    tidings they tell me.
Tidings—ah me, can it be then? that I, the
    blasphemer accounted,
Here am with reverent heed at the wondrous
    Analogy working,
Pondering thy words and thy gestures, whilst
    thou, a prophet apostate,
(How are the mighty fallen!) whilst thou, a shep-
    herd travestie,
(How are the mighty fallen!) with gun,—with
    pipe no longer,
Teachest the woods to re-echo thy game-killing
    recantations,
Teachest thy verse to exalt Amaryllis, a Countess's
    daughter?
  What, thou forgettest, bewildered, my Master,
    that rightly considered
Beauty must ever be useful, what truly is useful is
    graceful?
She that is handy is handsome, good dairy-maids
    must be good-looking,
If but the butter be nice, the tournure of the elbow
    is shapely,
If the cream-cheeses be white, far whiter the hands
    that made them,

If—but alas, is it true ? while the pupil alone in
    the cottage
Slowly elaborates here thy System of Feminine
    Graces,
Thou in the palace, its author, art dining, small-
    talking and dancing,
Dancing and pressing the fingers kid-gloved·of a
    Lady Maria.
  These are the final words, that came to the
    Tutor from Balloch.
I am conquered, it seems ! you will meet me, I
    hope, in Oxford,
Altered in manners and mind. I yield to the
    laws and arrangements,
Yield to the ancient existent decrees : who am I
    to resist them ?
Yes, you will find me altered in mind, I think, as
    in manners,
Anxious too to atone for six weeks' loss of your
    Logic.

  So in the cottage with Adam, the pupils five
    together,
Read, and bathed, and roamed, and thought not
    now of Philip,
All in the joy of their life, and glory of shooting-
    jackets.

VI

Ducite ab urbe domum, mea carmina, ducite Daphnin

BRIGHT October was come, the misty-bright
  October,
Bright October was come to burn and glen and
  cottage ;
But the cottage was empty, the *matutine* deserted.
  Who are these that walk by the shore of the
  salt sea water ?
Here in the dusky eve, on the road by the salt
  sea water ?
  Who are these ? and where ? it is no sweet
  seclusion ;
Blank hill-sides slope down to a salt sea loch at
  their bases,
Scored by runnels, that fringe ere they end with
  rowan and alder ;
Cottages here and there outstanding bare on the
  mountain,
Peat-roofed, windowless, white ; the road under-
  neath by the water.
  There on the blank hill-side, looking down
  through the loch to the ocean,
There with a runnel beside, and pine-trees twain
  before it,
There with the road underneath, and in sight of
  coaches and steamers,
Dwelling of David Mackaye, and his daughters
  Elspie and Bella,
Sends up a column of smoke the Bothie of Tober-
  na-vuolich.

And of the older twain, the elder was telling
    the younger,
How on his pittance of soil he lived, and raised
    potatoes,
Barley, and oats, in the bothie where lived his
    father before him ;
Yet was smith by trade, and had travelled making
    horse-shoes
Far ; in the army had seen some service with
    brave Sir Hector,
Wounded soon, and discharged, disabled as smith
    and soldier ;
He had been many things since that,—drover,
    schoolmaster,
Whitesmith,—but when his brother died childless
    came up hither ;
And although he could get fine work that would
    pay in the city,
Still was fain to abide where his father abode
    before him.
And the lassies are bonnie,—I'm father and
    mother to them,—
Bonnie and young ; they're healthier here, I judge,
    and safer,
I myself find time for their reading, writing, and
    learning.
    So on the road they walk by the shore of the
    salt sea water,
Silent a youth and maid, and elders twain con-
    versing.
    This was the letter that came when Adam was
    leaving the cottage.

If you can manage to see me before going off to
 Dartmoor,
Come by Tuesday's coach through Glencoe (you
 have not seen it),
Stop at the ferry below, and ask your way (you
 will wonder,
There however I am) to the Bothie of Tober-na-
 vuolich.
 And on another scrap, of next day's date, was
  written :—
It was by accident purely I lit on the place ; I was
 returning,
Quietly, travelling homeward by one of these
 wretched coaches ;
One of the horses cast a shoe ; and a farmer passing
Said, Old David's your man ; a clever fellow at
 shoeing
Once ; just here by the firs ; they call it Tober-
 na-vuolich.
So I saw and spoke with David Mackaye, our
 acquaintance.
When we came to the journey's end some five
 miles farther,
In my unoccupied evening I walked back again to
 the bothie.
 But on a final crossing, still later in date, was
  added :
Come as soon as you can ; be sure and do not
 refuse me.
Who would have guessed I should find my haven
 and end of my travel,
Here, by accident too, in the bothie we laughed
 about so ?

Who would have guessed that here would be she
    whose glance at Rannoch
Turned me in that mysterious way ; yes, angels
    conspiring,
Slowly drew me, conducted me, home, to herself ;
    the needle
Which in the shaken compass flew hither and
    thither, at last, long
Quivering, poises to north.   I think so.   But I
    am cautious :
More, at least, than I was in the old silly days
    when I left you.
    Not at the bothie now ; at the changehouse in
    the clachan ; [1]
Why I delay my letter is more than I can tell
    you.

    There was another scrap, without or date or
    comment,
Dotted over with various observations, as follows :
Only think, I had danced with her twice, and did
    not remember.
I was as one that sleeps on the railway ; one, who
    dreaming
Hears thro' his dream the name of his home shouted
    out ; hears and hears not,—
Faint, and louder again, and less loud, dying in
    distance ;
Dimly conscious, with something of inward debate
    and choice,—and
Sense of claim and reality present, anon relapses

[1] Public-house in the hamlet.

Nevertheless, and continues the dream and fancy, while forward
Swiftly, remorseless, the car presses on, he knows not whither.
  Handsome who handsome is, who handsome does is more so ;
Pretty is all very pretty, it's prettier far to be useful.
No, fair Lady Maria, I say not that ; but I *will* say,
Stately is service accepted, but lovelier service rendered,
Interchange of service the law and condition of beauty :
Any way beautiful only to be the thing one is meant for.
I, I am sure, for the sphere of mere ornament am not intended :
No, nor she, I think, thy sister at Tober-na-vuolich.
This was the letter of Philip, and this had brought the Tutor :
This is why Tutor and pupil are walking with David and Elspie.—
  When for the night they part, and these, once more together,
Went by the lochside along to the changehouse near in the clachan,
Thus to his pupil anon commenced the grave man, Adam.
  Yes, she is beautiful, Philip, beautiful even as morning :

Yes, it is that which I said, the Good and not the
    Attractive !
Happy is he that finds, and finding does not leave
    it !
    Ten more days did Adam with Philip abide at
      the changehouse,
Ten more nights they met, they walked with father
    and daughter.
Ten more nights, and night by night more distant
    away were
Philip and she ; every night less heedful, by habit,
    the father.
Happy ten days, most happy : and, otherwise than
    intended,
Fortunate visit of Adam, companion and friend to
    David.
Happy ten days, be ye fruitful of happiness ! Pass
    o'er them slowly,
Slowly ; like cruse of the prophet be multiplied,
    even to ages !
Pass slowly o'er them, ye days of October ; ye
    soft misty mornings,
Long dusky eves ; pass slowly ; and thou, great
    Term-time of Oxford
Awful with lectures and books, and Little-goes, and
    Great-goes,
Till but the sweet bud be perfect, recede and
    retire for the lovers,
Yea, for the sweet love of lovers, postpone thyself
    even to doomsday !
    Pass o'er them slowly, ye hours ! Be with
    them, ye Loves and Graces !

Indirect and evasive no longer, a cowardly
  bather,
Clinging to bough and to rock, and sidling along
  by the edges,
In your faith, ye Muses and Graces, who love the
  plain present,
Scorning historic abridgment and artifice anti-
  poetic,
In your faith, ye Muses and Loves, ye Loves and
  Graces,
I will confront the great peril, and speak with the
  mouth of the lovers,
As they spoke by the alders, at evening, the
  runnel below them,
Elspie, a diligent knitter, and Philip her fingers
  watching.

VII

Vesper adest, juvenes, consurgite : Vesper Olympo
Expectata diu vix tandem lumina tollit

FOR she confessed, as they sat in the dusk, and
  he saw not her blushes,
Elspie confessed at the sports long ago with her
  father she saw him,
When at the door the old man had told him the
  name of the bothie ;
Then after that at the dance ; yet again at a dance
  in Rannoch—
And she was silent, confused. Confused much
  rather Philip
Buried his face in his hands, his face that with
  blood was bursting.

Silent, confused, yet by pity she conquered her
    fear, and continued.
Katie is good and not silly; be comforted, Sir,
    about her;
Katie is good and not silly; tender, but not, like
    many,
Carrying off, and at once, for fear of being seen,
    in the bosom
Locking-up as in a cupboard the pleasure that any
    man gives them,
Keeping it out of sight as a prize they need be
    ashamed of;
That is the way, I think, Sir, in England more
    than in Scotland;
No, she lives and takes pleasure in all, as in
    beautiful weather,
Sorry to lose it, but just as we would be to lose
    fine weather.
And she is strong to return to herself and feel
    undeserted,
Oh, she is strong, and not silly: she thinks no
    further about you;
She has had kerchiefs before from gentle, I know,
    as from simple.
Yes, she is good and not silly; yet were you
    wrong, Mr. Philip,
Wrong, for yourself perhaps more than for her.
                But Philip replied not,
Raised not his eyes from the hands on his knees.
                And Elspie continued.
That was what gave me much pain, when I met
    you that dance at Rannoch,

Dancing myself too with you, while Katie danced
    with Donald ;
That was what gave me such pain ; I thought it
    all a mistaking,
All a mere chance, you know, and accident,—not
    proper choosing,—
There were at least five or six—not there, no,
    that I don't say,
But in the country about—you might just as well
    have been courting
That was what gave me much pain, and (you
    won't remember that, though),
Three days after, I met you, beside my uncle's,
    walking,
And I was wondering much, and hoped you
    wouldn't notice,
So as I passed I couldn't help looking.   You
    didn't know me.
But I was glad, when I heard next day you were
    gone to the teacher.
    And uplifting his face at last, with eyes dilated,
Large as great stars in mist, and dim, with
    dabbled lashes,
Philip, with new tears starting,
                You think I do not remember,
Said,—suppose that I did not observe !   Ah me,
    shall I tell you ?
Elspie, it was your look that sent me away from
    Rannoch.
It was your glance, that, descending, an instant
    revelation,
Showed me where I was, and whitherward going ;
    recalled me,

Sent me, not to my books, but to wrestlings of
    thought in the mountains.
Yes, I have carried your glance within me un-
    dimmed, unaltered,
As a lost boat the compass some passing ship has
    lent her,
Many a weary mile on road, and hill, and moor-
    land :
And you suppose that I do not remember, I had
    not observed it !
O, did the sailor bewildered observe when they
    told him his bearings ?
O, did he cast overboard, when they parted, the
    compass they gave him ?
  And he continued more firmly, although with
    stronger emotion :
  Elspie, why should I speak it ? you cannot
    believe it, and should not :
Why should I say that I love, which I all but said
    to another ?
Yet should I dare, should I say, O Elspie, you
    only I love ; you,
First and sole in my life that has been and surely
    that shall be ;
Could—O, could you believe it, O Elspie, believe
    it and spurn not ?
Is it—possible,—possible, Elspie ?
                    Well,—she answered,
And she was silent some time, and blushed all
    over, and answered
Quietly, after her fashion, still knitting, Maybe,
    I think of it,

Though I don't know that I did : and she paused
    again ; but it may be,
Yes,—I don't know, Mr. Philip,—but only it feels
    to me strangely,
Like to the high new bridge, they used to build
    at, below there,
Over the burn and glen on the road.   You won't
    understand me.
But I keep saying in my mind—this long time
    slowly with trouble
I have been building myself, up, up, and toilfully
    raising,
Just like as if the bridge were to do it itself with-
    out masons,
Painfully getting myself upraised one stone on
    another,
All one side I mean ; and now I see on the other
Just such another fabric uprising, better and
    stronger,
Close to me, coming to join me : and then I some-
    times fancy,—
Sometimes I find myself dreaming at nights about
    arches and bridges,—
Sometimes I dream of a great invisible hand
    coming down, and
Dropping the great key-stone in the middle : there
    in my dreaming,
There I felt the great key-stone coming in, and
    through it
Feel the other part—all the other stones of the
    archway,
Joined into mine with a strange happy sense of
    completeness.   But, dear me,

This is confusion and nonsense. I mix all the
    things I can think of.
And you won't understand, Mr. Philip.
                        But while she was speaking,
So it happened, a moment she paused from her
    work, and pondering,
Laid her hand on her lap : Philip took it : she
    did not resist :
So he retained her fingers, the knitting being
    stopped. But emotion
Came all over her more and yet more from his
    hand, from her heart, and
Most from the sweet idea and image her brain
    was renewing.
So he retained her hand, and, his tears down-
    dropping on it,
Trembling a long time, kissed it at last. And
    she ended.
And as she ended, uprose he : saying, What have
    I heard ? Oh,
What have I done, that such words should be said
    to me ? Oh, I see it,
See the great key-stone coming down from the
    heaven of heavens ;
And he fell at her feet, and buried his face in her
    apron.
  But as under the moon and stars they went to
    the cottage,
Elspie sighed and said, Be patient, dear Mr.
    Philip,
Do not do anything hasty. It is all so soon, so
    sudden.
Do not say anything yet to any one.

Elspie, he answered,
Does not my friend go on Friday? I then shall
see nothing of you.
Do not I go myself on Monday?
But oh, he said, Elspie!
Do as I bid you, my child: do not go on calling
me Mr.;
Might I not just as well be calling you Miss
Elspie?
Call me, this heavenly night for once, for the first
time, Philip.
Philip, she said, and laughed, and said she
could not say it;
Philip, she said; he turned, and kissed the sweet
·lips as they said it.

But on the morrow Elspie kept out of the way
of Philip:
And at the evening seat, when he took her hand
by the alders,
Drew it back, saying, almost peevishly,
No, Mr. Philip,
I was quite right, last night; it is too soon, too
sudden.
What I told you before was foolish perhaps, was
hasty.
When I think it over, I am shocked and terrified
at it.
Not that at all I unsay it; that is, I know I said
it,
And when I said it, felt it. But oh, we must wait,
Mr. Philip!

We mustn't pull ourselves at the great key-stone
    of the centre :
Some one else up above must hold it, fit it, and
    fix it ;
If we try ourselves, we shall only damage the
    archway,
Damage all our own work that we wrought, our
    painful upbuilding.
When, you remember, you took my hand last
    evening, talking,
I was all over a tremble : and as you pressed the
    fingers
After, and afterwards kissed them, I could not
    speak.   And then, too,
As we went home, you kissed me for saying your
    name.   It was dreadful.
I have been kissed before, she added, blushing
    slightly,
I have been kissed more than once by Donald my
    cousin, and others ;
It is the way of the lads, and I make up my mind
    not to mind it ;
But, Mr. Philip, last night, and from you, it was
    different, quite, Sir.
When I think of all that, I am shocked and
    terrified at it.
Yes, it is dreadful to me.
              She paused, but quickly continued,
Smiling almost fiercely, continued, looking upward.
You are too strong, you see, Mr. Philip ! just like
    the sea there,
Which *will* come, through the straits and all
    between the mountains

Forcing its great strong tide into every nook and
    inlet,
Getting far in, up the quiet stream of sweet inland
    water,
Sucking it up, and stopping it, turning it, driving
    it backward,
Quite preventing its own quiet running : and then,
    soon after,
Back it goes off, leaving weeds on the shore, and
    wrack and uncleanness :
And the poor burn in the glen tries again its
    peaceful running,
But it is brackish and tainted, and all its banks in
    disorder.
That was what I dreamt all last night.   I was the
    burnie,
Trying to get along through the tyrannous brine,
    and could not :
I was confined and squeezed in the coils of the
    great salt tide, that
Would mix-in itself with me, and change me ; I
    felt myself changing ;
And I struggled, and screamed, I believe, in my
    dream.   It was dreadful.
You are too strong, Mr. Philip !   I am but a poor
    slender burnie,
Used to the glens and the rocks, the rowan and
    birch of the woodies,
Quite unused to the great salt sea ; quite afraid
    and unwilling.
    Ere she had spoken two words, had Philip
    released her fingers ;

As she went on, he recoiled, fell back, and shook
    and shivered ;
There he stood, looking pale and ghastly ; when
    she had ended,
Answering in hollow voice,
                    It is true ; oh, quite true, Elspie ;
Oh, you are always right ; oh, what, what have I
    been doing ?
I will depart to-morrow.　But oh, forget me not
    wholly,
Wholly, Elspie, nor hate me ; no, do not hate me,
    my Elspie.
    But a revulsion passed through the brain and
    bosom of Elspie ;
And she got up from her seat on the rock, putting
    by her knitting ;
Went to him, where he stood, and answered :
                    No, Mr. Philip,
No, you are good, Mr. Philip, and gentle ; and I
    am the foolish :
No, Mr. Philip, forgive me.
             She stepped right to him, and boldly
Took up his hand, and placed it in hers : he dared
    no movement ;
Took up the cold hanging hand, up-forcing the
    heavy elbow.
I am afraid, she said, but I will ; and kissed the
    fingers.
And he fell on his knees and kissed her own past
    counting.

    But a revulsion wrought in the brain and bosom
    of Elspie ;

And the passion she just had compared to the
   vehement ocean,
Urging in high spring-tide its masterful way
   through the mountains,
Forcing and flooding the silvery stream, as it runs
   from the inland ;
That great power withdrawn, receding here and
   passive,
Felt she in myriad springs, her sources far in the
   mountains,
Stirring, collecting, rising, upheaving, forth-out-
   flowing,
Taking and joining, right welcome, that delicate
   rill in the valley,
Filling it, making it strong, and still descending,
   seeking,
With a blind forefeeling descending ever, and
   seeking,
With a delicious forefeeling, the great still sea
   before it ;
There deep into it, far, to carry, and lose in its
   bosom,
Waters that still from their sources exhaustless
   are fain to be added.
   As he was kissing her fingers, and knelt on the
      ground before her,
Yielding backward she sank to her seat, and of
   what she was doing
Ignorant, bewildered, in sweet multitudinous vague
   emotion,
Stooping, knowing not what, put her lips to the
   hair on his forehead :

And Philip, raising himself, gently, for the first
    time round her
Passing his arms, close, close, enfolded her, close
    to his bosom.
As they went home by the moon, Forgive me,
    Philip, she whispered ;
I have so many things to think of, all of a sudden ;
I who had never once thought a thing,—in my
    ignorant Highlands.

VIII

Jam veniet virgo, jam dicetur Hymenæus

BUT a revulsion again came over the spirit of
    Elspie,
When she thought of his wealth, his birth and
    education :
Wealth indeed but small, though to her a difference
    truly ;
Father nor mother had Philip, a thousand pounds
    his portion,
Somewhat impaired in a world where nothing is
    had for nothing ;
Fortune indeed but small, and prospects plain and
    simple.
    But the many things that he knew, and the
      ease of a practised
Intellect's motion, and all those indefinable
    graces
(Were they not hers, too, Philip ?) to speech, and
    manner, and movement,

Lent by the knowledge of self, and wisely in-
    structed feeling,—
When she thought of these, and these contemplated
    daily,
Daily appreciating more, and more exactly ap-
    praising,—
With these thoughts, and the terror withal of a
    thing she could not
Estimate, and of a step (such a step!) in the
    dark to be taken,
Terror nameless and ill-understood of deserting
    her station,—
Daily heavier, heavier upon her pressed the
    sorrow,
Daily distincter, distincter within her arose the
    conviction,
He was too high, too perfect, and she so unfit, so
    unworthy
(Ah me! Philip, that ever a word such as that
    should be written!),
It would do neither for him nor for her; she also
    was something,
Not much indeed, it was true, yet not to be
    lightly extinguished.
Should *he—he*, she said, have a wife beneath him!
    herself be
An inferior there where only equality can be?
It would do neither for him nor for her.
                     Alas for Philip!
Many were tears and great was perplexity. Nor
    had availed then
All his prayer and all his device. But much was
    spoken

Now, between Adam and Elspie: companions
 were they hourly:
Much by Elspie to Adam, inquiring, anxiously
 seeking,
From his experience seeking impartial accurate
 statement
What it was to do this or do that, go hither or
 thither,
How in the after-life would seem what now seem-
 ing certain
Might so soon be reversed; in her quest and
 obscure exploring
Still from that quiet orb soliciting light to her
 footsteps;
Much by Elspie to Adam, inquiringly, eagerly
 seeking:
Much by Adam to Elspie, informing, reassuring,
Much that was sweet to Elspie, by Adam heed-
 fully speaking,
Quietly, indirectly, in general terms, of Philip,
Gravely, but indirectly, not as incognisant wholly,
But as suspending until she should seek it, direct
 intimation;
Much that was sweet in her heart of what he was
 and would be,
Much that was strength to her mind, confirming
 beliefs and insights
Pure and unfaltering, but young and mute and
 timid for action:
Much of relations of rich and poor, and of true
 education.
  It was on Saturday eve, in the gorgeous bright
  October,

Then when brackens are changed, and heather
    blooms are faded,
And amid russet of heather and fern green trees
    are bonnie ;
Alders are green, and oaks ; the rowan scarlet
    and yellow ;
One great glory of broad gold pieces appears the
    aspen,
And the jewels of gold that were hung in the hair
    of the birch-tree,
Pendulous, here and there, her coronet, necklace,
    and ear-rings,
Cover her now, o'er and o'er ; she is weary and
    scatters them from her.
There, upon Saturday eve, in the gorgeous bright
    October,
Under the alders knitting, gave 'Elspie her troth
    to Philip,
For as they talked, anon she said,
                 It is well, Mr. Philip.
Yes, it is well : I have spoken, and learnt a deal
    with the teacher.
At the last I told him all, I could not help it ;
And it came easier with him than could have been
    with my father ;
And he calmly approved, as one that had fully
    considered.
Yes, it is well, I have hoped, though quite too
    great and sudden ;
I am so fearful, I think it ought not to be for
    years yet.
I am afraid ; but believe in you ; and I trust to
    the teacher ;

You have done all things gravely and temperate,
    not as in passion ;
And the teacher is prudent, and surely can tell
    what is likely.
What my father will say, I know not ; we will
    obey him :
But for myself, I could dare to believe all well,
    and venture.
O Mr. Philip, may it never hereafter seem to be
    different !
And she hid her face—
                Oh, where, but in Philip's bosom !

After some silence, some tears too perchance,
    Philip laughed, and said to her,
  So, my own Elspie, at last you are clear that
    I'm bad enough for you.
Ah ! but your father won't make one half the
    question about it
You have—he'll think me, I know, nor better nor
    worse than Donald,
Neither better nor worse for my gentlemanship
    and bookwork,
Worse, I fear, as he knows me an idle and vaga-
    bond fellow,
Though he allows, but he'll think it was all for
    your sake, Elspie,
Though he allows I did some good at the end of
    the shearing.
But I had thought in Scotland you didn't care for
    this folly.
How I wish, he said, you had lived all your days
    in the Highlands !

This is what comes of the year you spent in our
    foolish England.
You do not all of you feel these fancies.
                      No, she answered.
And in her spirit the freedom and ancient joy was
    reviving.
No, she said, and uplifted herself, and looked for
    her knitting,
No, nor do *I*, dear Philip, I don't myself feel
    always
As I have felt, more sorrow for me, these four
    days lately,
Like the Peruvian Indians I read about last winter,
Out in America there, in somebody's life of Pizarro;
Who were as good perhaps as the Spaniards; only
    weaker;
And that the one big tree might spread its root
    and branches,
All the lesser about it must even be felled and
    perish.
No, I feel much more as if I, as well as you, were,
Somewhere, a leaf on the one great tree, that, up
    from old time
Growing, contains in itself the whole of the virtue
    and life of
Bygone days, drawing now to itself all kindreds
    and nations
And must have for itself the whole world for its
    root and branches.
No, I belong to the tree, I shall not decay in the
    shadow;
Yes, and I feel the life-juices of all the world and
    the ages,

Coming to me as to you, more slowly no doubt
    and poorer :
You are more near, but then you will help to
    convey them to me.
No, don't smile, Philip, now, so scornfully! While
    you look so
Scornful and strong, I feel as if I were standing
    and trembling,
Fancying the burn in the dark a wide and rush-
    ing river ; .
And I feel coming unto me from you, or it may
    be from elsewhere,
Strong contemptuous resolve ; I forget, and I
    bound as across it.
But after all, you know, it may be a dangerous
    river.
    Oh, if it were so, Elspie, he said, I can carry
    you over.
Nay, she replied, you would tire of having me
    for a burden.
    O sweet burden, he said, and are you not light
    as a feather ?
But it is deep, very likely, she said, over head and
    ears too.
    O let us try, he answered, the waters themselves
    will support us,
Yea, very ripples and waves will form to a boat
    underneath us ;
There is a boat, he said, and a name is written
    upon it,
Love, he said, and kissed her.—
                But I will read your books, though,
Said she : you'll leave me some, Philip ?

                  Not I, replied he, a volume.
This is the way with you all, I perceive, high and
    low together.
Women must read, as if they didn't know all before-
    hand:
Weary of plying the pump, we turn to the running
    water,
And the running spring will needs have a pump
    built upon it.
Weary and sick of our books, we come to repose
    in your eyelight,
As to the woodland and water, the freshness and
    beauty of Nature.
Lo, you will talk, forsooth, of things we are sick
    to the death of.
    What, she said, and if I have let you become
      my sweetheart,
I am to read no books! but you may go your
    ways then,
And I will read, she said, with my father at home
    as I used to.
    If you must have it, he said, I myself will read
      them to you.
    Well, she said, but no, I will read to myself,
      when I choose it;
What, you suppose we never read anything here
    in our Highlands,
Bella and I with the father, in all our winter
    evenings!
But we must go, Mr. Philip—
                I shall not go at all, said
He, if you call me Mr.   Thank heaven! that's
    over for ever.

No, but it's not, she said, it is not over, nor
  will be.
Was it not then, she asked, the name I called you
    first by?
No, Mr. Philip, no—you have kissed me enough
    for two nights;
No—come, Philip, come, or I'll go myself without
    you.
  You never call me Philip, he answered, until I
    kiss you.
  As they went home by the moon that waning
    now rose later,
Stepping through mossy stones by the runnel
    under the alders,
Loitering unconsciously, Philip, she said, I will
    not be a lady;
We will do work together—you do not wish me a
    lady.
It is a weakness perhaps and a foolishness; still
    it is so;
I have been used all my life to help myself and
    others;
I could not bear to sit and be waited on by footmen,
No, not even by women—
                    And God forbid, he answered,
God forbid you should ever be aught but yourself,
    my Elspie !
As for service, I love it not, I ; your weakness is
    mine too,
I am sure Adam told you as much as that about
    me.
  I am sure, she said, he called you wild and
    flighty.

That was true, he said, till my wings were
　　clipped.　But, my Elspie,
You will at least just go and see my uncle and
　　cousins,
Sister, and brother, and brother's wife.　You
　· should go, if you liked it,
Just as you are ; just what you are, at any rate,
　　my Elspie.
Yes, we will go, and give the old solemn gentility
　　stage-play
One little look, to leave it with all the more
　　satisfaction.
　　That may be, my Philip, she said ; you are
　　good to think of it.
But we are letting our fancies run on indeed ; after
　　all, it
May all come, you know, Mr. Philip, to nothing
　　whatever,
There is so much that needs to be done, so much
　　that may happen.
　　All that needs to be done, said he, shall be
　　done, and quickly.
　　And on the morrow he took good heart, and
　　spoke with David.
Not unwarned the father, nor had been unperceiv-
　　ing :
Fearful much, but in all from the first reassured
　　by the Tutor.
And he remembered how he had fancied the lad
　　from the first ; and
Then, too, the old man's eye was much more for
　　inner than outer,

And the natural tune of his heart without mis-
    giving
Went to the noble words of that grand song of the
    Lowlands,
Rank is the guinea stamp, but the man's a man for
*   a' that.*
  Still he was doubtful, would hear nothing of it
    now, but insisted
Philip should go to his books ; if he chose, he
    might write ; if after
Chose to return, might come ; he truly believed
    him honest.
But a year must elapse, and many things might
    happen.
Yet at the end he burst into tears, called Elspie,
    and blessed them :
Elspie, my bairn, he said, I thought not when at
    the doorway
Standing with you, and telling the young man
    where he would find us,
I did not think he would one day be asking me
    here to surrender
What is to me more than wealth in my Bothie of
    Tober-na-vuolich.

IX

Arva, beata Petamus arva !

So on the morrow's morrow, with Term-time dread
    returning,
Philip returned to his books, and read, and remained
    at Oxford,

H

All the Christmas and Easter remained and read
    at Oxford.
    Great was wonder in College when postman
       showed to butler
Letters addressed to David Mackaye, at Tober-na-
    vuolich,
Letter on letter, at least one a week, one every
    Sunday :
    Great at that Highland post was wonder too and
       conjecture,
When the postman showed letters to wife, and wife
    to the lassies,
And the lassies declared they couldn't be really to
    David ;
Yes, they could see inside a paper with E. upon
    it.
    Great was surmise in College at breakfast, wine,
       and supper,
Keen the conjecture and joke ; but Adam kept the
    secret,
Adam the secret kept, and Philip read like fury.
    This is a letter written by Philip at Christmas
       to Adam.
There may be beings, perhaps, whose vocation it
    is to be idle,
Idle, sumptuous even, luxurious, if it must be :
Only let each man seek to be that for which nature
    meant him.
If you were meant to plough, Lord Marquis, out
    with you, and do it ;
If you were meant to be idle, O beggar, behold, I
    will feed you.

If you were born for a groom, and you seem, by
    your dress, to believe so,
Do it like a man, Sir George, for pay, in a livery
    stable ;
Yes, you may so release that slip of a boy at the
    corner,
Fingering books at the window, misdoubting the
    eighth commandment.
Ah, fair Lady Maria, God meant you to live and
    be lovely ;
Be so then, and I bless you. But ye, ye spurious
    ware, who
Might be plain women, and can be by no possibility
    better !
—Ye unhappy statuettes, and miserable trinkets,
Poor alabaster chimney-piece ornaments under
    glass cases,
Come, in God's name, come down ! the very
    French clock by you
Puts you to shame with ticking ; the fire-irons
    deride you.
You, young girl, who have had such advantages,
    learnt so quickly,
Can you not teach ?   O yes, and she likes Sunday-
    school extremely,
Only it's soon in the morning.   Away ! if to teach
    be your calling,
It is no play, but a business : off ! go teach and
    be paid for it.
Lady Sophia's so good to the sick, so firm and so
    gentle.
Is there a nobler sphere than of hospital nurse and
    matron ?

Hast thou for cooking a turn, little Lady Clarissa ?
in with them,
In with your fingers ! their beauty it spoils, but
your own it enhances,
For it is beautiful only to do the thing we are
meant for.
This was the answer that came from the Tutor,
the grave man, Adam.
When the armies are set in array, and the battle
beginning,
Is it well that the soldier whose post is far to the
leftward
Say, I will go to the right, it is there I shall do
best service ?
There is a great Field-Marshal, my friend, who
arrays our battalions ;
Let us to Providence trust, and abide and work in
our stations.
This was the final retort from the eager, im-
petuous Philip.
I am sorry to say your Providence puzzles me
sadly ;
Children of Circumstance are we to be ? you answer,
On no wise !
Where does Circumstance end, and Providence,
where begins it ?
What are we to resist, and what are we to be friends
with ?
If there is battle, 'tis battle by night, I stand in
the darkness,
Here in the mêlée of men, Ionian and Dorian on
both sides,

Signal and password known ; which is friend and
which is foeman ?
Is it a friend ?   I doubt, though he speak with the
voice of a brother.
Still you are right, I suppose ; you always are, and
will be ;
Though I mistrust the Field-Marshal, I bow to the
duty of order.
Yet is my feeling rather to ask, where *is* the battle ?
Yes, I could find in my heart to cry, notwithstand-
ing my Elspie,
O that the armies indeed were arrayed !   O joy
of the onset !
Sound, thou Trumpet of God, come forth, Great
Cause, to array us,
King and leader appear, thy soldiers sorrowing
seek thee.
Would that the armies indeed were arrayed, O
where is the battle !
Neither battle I see, nor arraying, nor King in
Israel,
Only infinite jumble and mess and dislocation,
Backed by a solemn appeal, ' For God's sake, do
not stir, there ! '
Yet you are right, I suppose ; if you don't attack
my conclusion,
Let us get on as we can, and do the thing we are
fit for ;
Every one for himself, and the common success
for us all, and
Thankful, if not for our own, why then for the
triumph of others,

Get along, each as we can, and do the thing we
    are meant for.
That isn't likely to be by sitting still, eating and
    drinking.
    These are fragments again without date ad-
      dressed to Adam.
As at return of tide the total weight of ocean,
Drawn by moon and sun from Labrador and
    Greenland,
Sets-in amain, in the open space betwixt Mull
    and Scarba,
Heaving, swelling, spreading the might of the
    mighty Atlantic ;
There into cranny and slit of the rocky, cavernous
    bottom
Settles down, and with dimples huge the smooth
    sea-surface
Eddies, coils, and whirls ; by dangerous Corry-
    vreckan :
So in my soul of souls, through its cells and secret
    recesses,
Comes back, swelling and spreading, the old
    democratic fervour.
    But as the light of day enters some populous
    city,
Shaming away, ere it come, by the chilly day-
    streak signal,
High and low, the misusers of night, shaming out
    the gas-lamps—
All the great empty streets are flooded with
    broadening clearness,
Which, withal, by inscrutable simultaneous access

Permeates far and pierces to the very cellars
lying in
Narrow high back-lane, and court, and alley of
alleys :—
He that goes forth to his walks, while speeding
to the suburb,
Sees sights only peaceful and pure : as labourers
settling
Slowly to work, in their limbs the lingering sweetness of slumber ;
Humble market-carts, coming in, bringing in, not
only
Flower, fruit, farm-store, but sounds and sights of
the country
Dwelling yet on the sense of the dreamy drivers ;
soon after
Half-awake servant-maids unfastening drowsy
shutters
Up at the windows, or down, letting-in the air by
the doorway ;
School-boys, school-girls soon, with slate, portfolio,
satchel,
Hampered as they haste, those running, these
others maidenly tripping ;
Early clerk anon turning out to stroll, or it may
be
Meet his sweetheart—waiting behind the garden
gate there ;
Merchant on his grass-plat haply bare-headed ;
and now by this time
Little child bringing breakfast to 'father' that sits
on the timber

There by the scaffolding ; see, she waits for the
  can beside him ;
Meantime above purer air untarnished of new-lit
  fires :
So that the whole great wicked artificial civilised
  fabric—
All its unfinished houses, lots for sale, and railway
  out-works—
Seems reaccepted, resumed to Primal Nature and
  Beauty :—
—Such—in me, and to me, and on me the love
  of Elspie !
  Philip returned to his books, but returned to
  his Highlands after ;
Got a first, 'tis said ; a winsome bride, 'tis certain.
There while courtship was ending, nor yet the
  wedding appointed,
Under her father he studied the handling of hoe
  and of hatchet :
Thither that summer succeeding came Adam and
  Arthur to see him
Down by the lochs from the distant Glenmorison ;
  Adam the Tutor,
Arthur, and Hope ; and the Piper anon who was
  there for a visit ;
He had been into the schools ; plucked almost ;
  all but a *gone-coon ;*
So he declared ; never once had brushed up his
  hairy Aldrich ;
Into the great might-have-been upsoaring sublime
  and ideal
Gave to historical questions a free poetical treat-
  ment ;

Leaving vocabular ghosts undisturbed in their
    lexicon-limbo,
Took Aristophanes up at a shot; and the whole
    three last weeks
Went, in his life and the sunshine rejoicing, to
    Nuneham and Godstowe :
What were the claims of Degree to those of life
    and the sunshine ?
There did the four find Philip, the poet, the
    speaker, the Chartist,
Delving at Highland soil, and railing at Highland
    landlords,
Railing, but more, as it seemed, for the fun of the
    Piper's fury.
There saw they David and Elspie Mackaye, and
    the Piper was almost,
Almost deeply in love with Bella the sister of
    Elspie ;
But the good Adam was heedful : they did not go
    too often.
There in the bright October, the gorgeous bright
    October,
When the brackens are changed, and heather
    blooms are faded,
And amid russet of heather and fern green trees
    are bonnie,
Alders are green, and oaks, the rowan scarlet and
    yellow,
Heavy the aspen, and heavy with jewels of gold
    the birch-tree,
There, when shearing had ended, and barley-
    stooks were garnered,

David gave Philip to wife his daughter, his darling
    Elspie ;
Elspie the quiet, the brave, was wedded to Philip
    the poet.
    So won Philip his bride.   They are married
       and gone—But oh, Thou
Mighty one, Muse of great Epos, and Idyll the
    playful and tender,
Be it recounted in song, ere we part, and thou fly
    to thy Pindus,
(Pindus is it, O Muse, or Ætna, or even Ben-
    nevis ?)
Be it recounted in song, O Muse of the Epos and
    Idyll,
Who gave what at the wedding, the gifts and fair
    gratulations.
    Adam, the grave careful Adam, a medicine
       chest and tool-box,
Hope a saddle, and Arthur a plough, and the
    Piper a rifle,
Airlie a necklace for Elspie, and Hobbes a Family
    Bible,
Airlie a necklace, and Hobbes a Bible and iron
    bedstead.
    What was the letter, O Muse, sent withal by
       the corpulent hero ?
This is the letter of Hobbes the kilted and
    corpulent hero.
    So the last speech and confession is made, O
       my eloquent speaker !
So *the good time* is *coming*, or come is it ? O
    my Chartist !

So the cathedral is finished at last, O my Pugin
of women ;
Finished, and now, is it true ? to be taken out
whole to New Zealand !
Well, go forth to thy field, to thy barley, with
Ruth, O Boaz,
Ruth, who for thee hath deserted her people, her
gods, her mountains.
Go, as in Ephrath of old, in the gate of Bethlehem
said they,
Go, be the wife in thy house both Rachel and
Leah unto thee ;
Be thy wedding of silver, albeit of iron thy bed-
stead !
Yea, to the full golden fifty renewed be ! and fair
memoranda
Happily fill the fly-leaves duly left in the Family
Bible.
Live, and when Hobbes is forgotten, may'st thou,
an unroasted Grandsire,
See thy children's children, and Democracy upon
New Zealand !
　This was the letter of Hobbes, and this the
postscript after.
Wit in the letter will prate, but wisdom speaks in
a postscript ;
Listen to wisdom—*Which things*—you perhaps
didn't know, my dear fellow,
I have reflected ; *Which things are an allegory*,
Philip.
For this Rachel-and-Leah is marriage ; which, I
have seen it,

Lo, and have known it, is always, and must be,
    bigamy only,
Even in noblest kind a duality, compound, and
    complex,
One part heavenly-ideal, the other vulgar and
    earthy:
For this Rachel-and-Leah is marriage, and Laban,
    their father,
Circumstance, chance, the world, our uncle and
    hard task-master.
Rachel we found as we fled from the daughters of
    Heth by the desert;
Rachel we met at the well; we came, we saw, we
    kissed her;
Rachel we serve-for, long years,—that seem as a
    few days only,
E'en for the love we have to her,—and win her at
    last of Laban.
Is it not Rachel we take in our joy from the hand
    of her father?
Is it not Rachel we lead in the mystical veil from
    the altar?
Rachel we dream-of at night: in the morning,
    behold, it is Leah.
'Nay, it is custom,' saith Laban, the Leah indeed
    is the elder.
Happy and wise who consents to redouble his
    service to Laban,
So, fulfilling her week, he may add to the elder
    the younger,
Not repudiates Leah, but wins the Rachel unto her!
Neither hate thou thy Leah, my Jacob, she also
    is worthy;

So, many days shall thy Rachel have joy, and
    survive her sister ;
Yea, and her children—*Which things are an
    allegory*, Philip,
Aye, and by Origen's head with a vengeance truly,
    a long one !
    This was a note from the Tutor, the grave man,
    nick-named Adam.
I shall see you of course, my Philip, before your
    departure.
Joy be with you, my boy, with you and your
    beautiful Elspie.
Happy is he that found, and finding was not
    heedless ;
Happy is he that found, and happy the friend
    that was with him.
    So won Philip his bride :—
        They are married and gone to New Zealand.
Five hundred pounds in pocket, with books, and
    two or three pictures,
Tool-box, plough, and the rest, they rounded the
    sphere to New Zealand.
There he hewed, and dug ; subdued the earth and
    his spirit ;
There he built him a home ; there Elspie bare
    him his children,
David and Bella ; perhaps ere this too an Elspie
    or Adam ;
There hath he farmstead and land, and fields of
    corn and flax fields ;
And the Antipodes too have a Bothie of Tober-na-
    vuolich.

EARLY POEMS

REVIVAL

SO I went wrong,
Grievously wrong, but folly crushed itself,
And vanity o'ertoppling fell, and time
And healthy discipline and some neglect,
Labour and solitary hours revived
Somewhat, at least, of that original frame.
Oh, well do I remember then the days
When on some grassy slope (what time the sun
Was sinking, and the solemn eve came down
With its blue vapour upon field and wood
And elm-embosomed spire) once more again
I fed on sweet emotion, and my heart
With love o'erflowed, or hushed itself in fear
Unearthly, yea celestial.   Once again
My heart was hot within me, and, me seemed,
I too had in my body breath to wind
The magic horn of song ; I too possessed
Up-welling in my being's depths a fount
Of the true poet-nectar whence to fill
The golden urns of verse.

1839

I

IN A LECTURE-ROOM

AWAY, haunt thou not me,
Thou vain Philosophy!
Little hast thou bestead,
Save to perplex the head,
And leave the spirit dead.
Unto thy broken cisterns wherefore go,
While from the secret treasure-depths below,
Fed by the skiey shower,
And clouds that sink and rest on hill-tops high,
Wisdom at once, and Power,
Are welling, bubbling forth, unseen, incessantly?
Why labour at the dull mechanic oar,
When the fresh breeze is blowing,
And the strong current flowing,
Right onward to the Eternal Shore?

1840

A SONG OF AUTUMN

My wind is turned to bitter north,
　That was so soft a south before ;
My sky, that shone so sunny bright,
　With foggy gloom is clouded o'er :
My gay green leaves are yellow-black,
　Upon the dank autumnal floor ;
For love, departed once, comes back
　No more again, no more.

A roofless ruin lies my home,
　For winds to blow and rains to pour ;
One frosty night befell, and lo !
　I find my summer days are o'er :
The heart bereaved, of why and how
　Unknowing, knows that yet before
It had what e'en to Memory now
　Returns no more, no more.

τὸ καλόν

I HAVE seen higher, holier things than these,
    And therefore must to these refuse my heart,
Yet am I panting for a little ease ;
    I'll take, and so depart.

Ah, hold ! the heart is prone to fall away,
    Her high and cherished visions to forget,
And if thou takest, how wilt thou repay
    So vast, so dread a debt ?

How will the heart, which now thou trustest,
      then
    Corrupt, yet in corruption mindful yet,
Turn with sharp stings upon itself ! Again,
    Bethink thee of the debt !

—Hast thou seen higher, holier things than
      these,
    And therefore must to these thy heart refuse ?
With the true best, alack, how ill agrees
    That best that thou would'st choose !

The Summum Pulchrum rests in heaven above ;
    Do thou, as best thou may'st, thy duty do :
Amid the things allowed thee live and love ;
    Some day thou shalt it view.

1841

Χρυσέα κλῄs ἐπὶ γλώσσᾳ

IF, when in cheerless wanderings, dull and cold,
A sense of human kindliness hath found us,
    We seem to have around us
    An atmosphere all gold,
'Midst darkest shades a halo rich of shine,
An element, that while the bleak wind bloweth,
    On the rich heart bestoweth
    Imbreathèd draughts of wine ;
Heaven guide, the cup be not, as chance may be,
To some vain mate given up as soon as tasted !
    No, nor on thee be wasted,
    Thou trifler, Poesy !
Heaven grant the manlier heart, that timely, ere
Youth fly, with life's real tempest would be coping;
    The fruit of dreamy hoping
    Is, waking, blank despair.

1841

THE MUSIC OF THE WORLD AND OF THE SOUL

I

WHY should I say I see the things I see not?
  Why be and be not?
Show love for that I love not, and fear for what I
    fear not?
And dance about to music that I hear not?
  Who standeth still i' the street
  Shall be hustled and justled about;
And he that stops i' the dance shall be spurned
    by the dancers' feet,—
Shall be shoved and be twisted by all he shall
    meet,
  And shall raise up an outcry and rout;
  And the partner, too,—
  What's the partner to do?
While all the while 'tis but, perchance, an hum-
    ming in mine ear,
  That yet anon shall hear,
  And I anon, the music in my soul,
  In a moment read the whole;
  The music in my heart,
  Joyously take my part,

And hand in hand, and heart with heart, with
    these retreat, advance ;
      And borne on wings of wavy sound,
      Whirl with these around, around,
Who here are living in the living dance !
      Why forfeit that fair chance ?
      Till that arrive, till thou awake,
      Of these, my soul, thy music make,
      And keep amid the throng,
And turn as they shall turn, and bound as they
    are bounding,—
Alas ! alas ! alas ! and what if all along
    The music is not sounding ?

II

Are there not, then, two musics unto men ?—
      One loud and bold and coarse,
      And overpowering still perforce
      All tone and tune beside ;
      Yet in despite its pride
Only of fumes of foolish fancy bred,
And sounding solely in the sounding head :
      The other, soft and low,
      Stealing whence we not know,
Painfully heard, and easily forgot,
With pauses oft and many a silence strange
(And silent oft it seems, when silent it is not),
Revivals too of unexpected change :
Haply thou think'st 'twill never be begun,
Or that 't has come, and been, and passed away :
      Yet turn to other none,—
      Turn not, oh, turn not thou !

But listen, listen, listen,—if haply be heard it may ;
Listen, listen, listen,—is it not sounding now ?

III

Yea, and as thought of some departed friend
By death or distance parted will descend,
Severing, in crowded rooms ablaze with light,
As by a magic screen, the seër from the sight
(Palsying the nerves that intervene
The eye and central sense between) ;
    So may the ear,
    Hearing not hear,
Though drums do roll, and pipes and cymbals
       ring ;
So the bare conscience of the better thing
Unfelt, unseen, unimaged, all unknown,
May fix the entrancèd soul 'mid multitudes alone.

QUA CURSUM VENTUS

As ships, becalmed at eve, that lay
  With canvas drooping, side by side,
Two towers of sail at dawn of day
  Are scarce long leagues apart descried ;

When fell the night, upsprung the breeze,
  And all the darkling hours they plied,
Nor dreamt but each the self-same seas
  By each was cleaving, side by side :

E'en so—but why the tale reveal
  Of those, whom year by year unchanged,
Brief absence joined anew to feel,
  Astounded, soul from soul estranged ?

At dead of night their sails were filled,
  And onward each rejoicing steered—
Ah, neither blame, for neither willed,
  Or wist, what first with dawn appeared !

To veer, how vain ! On, onward strain,
  Brave barks ! In light, in darkness too,
Through winds and tides one compass guides—
  To that, and your own selves, be true.

But O blithe breeze ; and O great seas,
    Though ne'er, that earliest parting past,
On your wide plain they join again,
    Together lead them home at last.

One port, methought, alike they sought,
    One purpose hold where'er they fare, —
O bounding breeze, O rushing seas !
    At last, at last, unite them there !

'WEN GOTT BETRÜGT, IST WOHL BETROGEN'

Is it true, ye gods, who treat us
As the gambling fool is treated ;
O ye, who ever cheat us,
And let us feel we're cheated !
Is it true that poetical power,
The gift of heaven, the dower
Of Apollo and the Nine,
The inborn sense, 'the vision and the faculty
 divine,'
All we glorify and bless   .
In our rapturous exaltation,
All invention, and creation,
Exuberance of fancy, and sublime imagination,
All a poet's fame is built on,
The fame of Shakespeare, Milton,
Of Wordsworth, Byron, Shelley,
Is in reason's grave precision,
Nothing more, nothing less,
Than a peculiar conformation,
Constitution, and condition
Of the brain and of the belly ?
Is it true, ye gods who cheat us ?
And that's the way ye treat us ?

Oh say it, all who think it,
Look straight, and never blink it !
If it is so, let it be so,
And we will all agree so ;
But the plot has counterplot,
It may be, and yet be not.

THE NEW SINAI

Lo, here is God, and there is God !
   Believe it not, O Man ;
In such vain sort to this and that
   The ancient heathen ran :
Though old Religion shake her head,
   And say in bitter grief,
The day behold, at first foretold,
   Of atheist unbelief :
Take better part, with manly heart,
   Thine adult spirit can ;
Receive it not, believe it not,
   Believe it not, O Man !

As men at dead of night awaked
   With cries, ' The king is here,'
Rush forth and greet whome'er they meet,
   Whoe'er shall first appear ;
And still repeat, to all the street,
   ' 'Tis he,—the king is here ;'
The long procession moveth on,
   Each nobler form they see,
With changeful suit they still salute
   And cry, ' 'Tis he, 'tis he !'

So, even so, when men were young,
    And earth and heaven were new,
And His immediate presence He
    From human hearts withdrew,
The soul perplexed and daily vexed
    With sensuous False and True,
Amazed, bereaved, no less believed,
    And fain would see Him too :
'He is !' the prophet-tongues proclaimed ;
    In joy and hasty fear,
'He is !' aloud replied the crowd,
    'Is here, and here, and here.'

'He is !   They are !' in distance seen
    On yon Olympus high,
In those Avernian woods abide,
    And walk this azure sky :
'They are !   They are !'—to every show
    Its eyes the baby turned,
And blazes sacrificial, tall,
    On thousand altars burned :
'They are !   They are !'—On Sinai's top
    Far seen the lightnings shone,
The thunder broke, a trumpet spoke,
    And God said, 'I am One.'

God spake it out, 'I, God, am One ;'
    The unheeding ages ran,
And baby-thoughts again, again,
    Have dogged the growing man :
And as of old from Sinai's top
    God said that God is One,

By Science strict so speaks He now
  To tell us, There is None !
Earth goes by chemic forces ; Heaven's
  A Mécanique Céleste !
And heart and mind of human kind
  A watch-work as the rest !

Is this a Voice, as was the Voice,
  Whose speaking told abroad,
When thunder pealed, and mountain reeled,
  The ancient truth of God ?
Ah, not the Voice ; 'tis but the cloud,
  The outer darkness dense,
Where image none, nor e'er was seen
  Similitude of sense.
'Tis but the cloudy darkness dense
  That wrapt the Mount around ;
While in amaze the people stays,
  To hear the Coming Sound.

Is there no prophet-soul the while
  To dare, sublimely meek,
Within the shroud of blackest cloud
  The Deity to seek ?
'Midst atheistic systems dark,
  And darker hearts' despair,
That soul has heard perchance His word,
  And on the dusky air
His skirts, as passed He by, to see
  Hath strained on their behalf,
Who on the plain, with dance amain,
  Adore the Golden Calf.

'Tis but the cloudy darkness dense ;
  Though blank the tale it tells,
No God, no Truth ! yet He, in sooth,
  Is there—within it dwells ;
Within the sceptic darkness deep
  He dwells that none may see,
Till idol forms and idol thoughts
  Have passed and ceased to be :
No God, no Truth ! ah though, in sooth
  So stand the doctrine's half :
On Egypt's track return not back,
  Nor own the Golden Calf.

Take better part, with manlier heart,
  Thine adult spirit can ;
No God, no Truth, receive it ne'er—
  Believe it ne'er—O Man !
But turn not then to seek again
  What first the ill began ;
No God, it saith ; ah, wait in faith
  God's self-completing plan ;
Receive it not, but leave it not,
  And wait it out, O Man !

' The Man that went the cloud within
  Is gone and vanished quite ;
He cometh not,' the people cries,
  ' Nor bringeth God to sight :
Lo these thy gods, that safety give,
  Adore and keep the feast !'
Deluding and deluded cries
  The Prophet's brother-Priest :

And Israel all bows down to fall
  Before the gilded beast.

Devout, indeed ! that priestly creed,
  O Man, reject as sin ;
The clouded hill attend thou still,
  And him that went within.
He yet shall bring some worthy thing
  For waiting souls to see :
Some sacred word that he hath heard
  Their light and life shall be ;
Some lofty part, than which the heart
  Adopt no nobler can,
Thou shalt receive, thou shalt believe
  And thou shalt do, O Man !

1845

THE QUESTIONING SPIRIT

THE human spirits saw I on a day,
Sitting and looking each a different way;
And hardly tasking, subtly questioning,
Another spirit went around the ring
To each and each : and as he ceased his say,
Each after each, I heard them singly sing,
Some querulously high, some softly, sadly low,
We know not—what avails to know?
We know not—wherefore need we know?
This answer gave they still unto his suing,
We know not, let us do as we are doing.
Dost thou not know that these things only seem ?—
I know not, let me dream my dream.
Are dust and ashes fit to make a treasure ?—
I know not, let me take my pleasure.
What shall avail the knowledge thou hast sought ?—
I know not, let me think my thought.
What is the end of strife ?—
I know not, let me live my life.
How many days or e'er thou mean'st to move ?—
I know not, let me love my love.
Were not things old once new ?—
I know not, let me do as others do.
And when the rest were over past,
I know not, I will do my duty, said the last

Thy duty do? rejoined the voice,
Ah, do it, do it, and rejoice;
But shalt thou then, when all is done,
Enjoy a love, embrace a beauty
Like these, that may be seen and won
In life, whose course will then be run;
Or wilt thou be where there is none?
I know not, I will do my duty.

And taking up the word around, above, below,
Some querulously high, some softly, sadly low,
We know not, sang they all, nor ever need we
    know;
We know not, sang they, what avails to know?
Whereat the questioning spirit, some short space,
Though unabashed, stood quiet in his place.
But as the echoing chorus died away
And to their dreams the rest returned apace,
By the one spirit I saw him kneeling low,
And in a silvery whisper heard him say:
Truly, thou know'st not, and thou need'st not
    know;
Hope only, hope thou, and believe alway;
I also know not, and I need not know,
Only with questionings pass I to and fro,
Perplexing these that sleep, and in their folly
Imbreeding doubt and sceptic melancholy;
Till that, their dreams deserting, they with me
Come all to this true ignorance and thee.

1847

BETHESDA

A SEQUEL

I SAW again the spirits on a day,
Where on the earth in mournful case they lay ;
Five porches were there, and a pool, and round,
Huddling in blankets, strewn upon the ground,
Tied-up and bandaged, weary, sore and spent,
The maimed and halt, diseased and impotent.
For a great angel came, 'twas said, and stirred
The pool at certain seasons, and the word
Was, with this people of the sick, that they
Who in the waters here their limbs should lay
Before the motion on the surface ceased
Should of their torment straightway be released.
So with shrunk bodies and with heads down-dropt,
Stretched on the steps, and at the pillars propt,
Watching by day and listening through the night,
They filled the place, a miserable sight.

And I beheld that on the stony floor
He too, that spoke of duty once before,
No otherwise than others here to-day,
Foredone and sick and sadly muttering lay.
' I know not, I will do—what is it I would say ?

What was that word which once sufficed alone for
    all,
Which now I seek in vain, and never can recall ? '
And then, as weary of in vain renewing
His question, thus his mournful thought pursuing,
' I know not, I must do as other men are doing.'

But what the waters of that pool might be,
Of Lethe were they, or Philosophy ;
And whether he, long waiting, did attain
Deliverance from the burden of his pain
There with the rest ; or whether, yet before,
Some more diviner stranger passed the door
With his small company into that sad place,
And breathing hope into the sick man's face,
Bade him take up his bed, and rise and go,
What the end were, and whether it were so,
Further than this I saw not, neither know.

1849

QUI LABORAT, ORAT

O ONLY Source of all our light and life,
  Whom as our truth, our strength, we see and feel,
But whom the hours of mortal moral strife
  Alone aright reveal !

Mine inmost soul, before Thee inly brought,
  Thy presence owns ineffable, divine ;
Chastised each rebel self-encentered thought,
  My will adoreth Thine.

With eye down-dropt, if then this earthly mind
  Speechless remain, or speechless e'en depart ;
Nor seek to see—for what of earthly kind
  Can see Thee as Thou art ?—

If well-assured 'tis but profanely bold
  In thought's abstractest forms to seem to see,
It dare not dare the dread communion hold
  In ways unworthy Thee,

O not unowned, thou shalt unnamed forgive,
  In worldly walks the prayerless heart prepare ;
And if in work its life it seem to live,
  Shalt make that work be prayer.

Nor times shall lack, when while the work it plies,
  Unsummoned powers the blinding film shall part,
And scarce by happy tears made dim, the eyes
  In recognition start.

But, as thou willest, give or e'en forbear
  The beatific supersensual sight,
So, with Thy blessing blest, that humbler prayer
  Approach Thee morn and night.

FROM 'DIPSYCHUS'

FROM 'DIPSYCHUS'[1]

The Piazza at Night

Dipsychus speaks. There have been times, not
    many, but enough
To quiet all repinings of the heart ;
There have been times, in which my tranquil soul,
No longer nebulous, sparse, errant, seemed
Upon its axis solidly to move,
Centred and fast : no mere elastic blank
For random rays to traverse unretained,
But rounding luminous its fair ellipse
Around its central sun.   Ay, yet again,
As in more faint sensations I detect,
With it too, round an Inner, Mightier orb,
Maybe with that too—this I dare not say—
Around, yet more, more central, more supreme,
Whate'er how numerous soe'er they be,
I am and feel myself, where'er I wind,
What vagrant chance soe'er I seem to obey
Communicably theirs.

[1] The blank verse extract is given out of its place, in
order to indicate the plan of the poem : the alternate utter-
ances of Dipsychus, the double-souled hesitating thinker,
and the practical cynic, called the Spirit, who deliver
themselves according to their kind, in the verses that follow.

O happy hours !
O compensation ample for long days
Of what impatient tongues called wretchedness !
O beautiful, beneath the magic moon,
To walk the watery way of palaces !
O beautiful, o'ervaulted with gemmed blue,
This spacious court, with colour and with gold,
With cupolas, and pinnacles, and points,
And crosses multiplex, and tips and balls
(Wherewith the bright stars unreproving mix,
Nor scorn by hasty eyes to be confused) ;
Fantastically perfect this low pile
Of Oriental glory ; these long ranges
Of classic chiselling, this gay flickering crowd,
And the calm Campanile.   Beautiful !
O beautiful ! and that seemed more profound,
This morning by the pillar when I sat
Under the great arcade, at the review,
And took, and held, and ordered on my brain
The faces, and the voices, and the whole mass
O' the motley facts of existence flowing by !
O perfect, if 'twere all !   But it is not ;
Hints haunt me ever of a more beyond :
I am rebuked by a sense of the incomplete,
Of a completion over soon assumed,
Of adding up too soon.   What we call sin,
I could believe a painful opening out
Of paths for ampler virtue.   The bare field,
Scant with lean ears of harvest, long had mocked
The vext laborious farmer ; came at length
The deep plough in the lazy undersoil
Down-driving ; with a cry earth's fibres crack,
And a few months, and lo ! the golden leas,

And autumn's crowded shocks and loaded wains.
Let us look back on life ; was any change,
Any now blest expansion, but at first
A pang, remorse-like, shot to the inmost seats
Of moral being ?   To do anything,
Distinct on any one thing to decide,
To leave the habitual and the old, and quit
The easy-chair of use and wont, seems crime
To the weak soul, forgetful how at first
Sitting down seemed so too.   And, oh ! this
    woman's heart,
Fain to be forced, incredulous of choice,
And waiting a necessity for God.
   Yet I could think, indeed, the perfect call
Should force the perfect answer.   If the voice
Ought to receive its echo from the soul,
Wherefore this silence ?   If it *should* rouse my
    being,
Why this reluctance ?   Have I not thought o'er
    much
Of other men, and of the ways of the world ?
But what they are, or have been, matters not.
To thine own self be true, the wise man says.
Are then my fears myself ?   O double self !
And I untrue to both ?   Oh, there are hours,
When love, and faith, and dear domestic ties,
And converse with old friends, and pleasant walks,
Familiar faces, and familiar books,
Study, and art, upliftings unto prayer,
And admiration of the noblest things,
Seem all ignoble only ; all is mean,
And nought as I would have it.   Then at others,
My mind is in her rest ; my heart at home

In all around ; my soul secure in place,
And the vext needle perfect to her poles.
Aimless and hopeless in my life I seem
To thread the winding byways of the town,
Bewildered, baffled, hurried hence and thence,
All at cross-purpose even with myself,
Unknowing whence or whither.   Thence at once,
At a step, I crown the Campanile's top,
And view all mapped below ; islands, lagoon,
A hundred steeples and a million roofs,
The fruitful champaign, and the cloud-capt Alps,
And the broad Adriatic.   Be it enough ;
If I lose this, how terrible !   No, no,
I am contented, and will not complain.
To the old paths, my soul !   Oh, be it so !
I bear the workday burden of dull life
About these footsore flags of a weary world,
Heaven knows how long it has not been ; at once,
Lo ! I am in the spirit on the Lord's day
With John in Patmos.   Is it not enough,
One day in seven ? and if this should go,
If this pure solace should desert my mind,
What were all else ?   I dare not risk this loss.
To the old paths, my soul !

   Spirit.   O yes.
To moon about religion ; to inhume
Your ripened age in solitary walks,
For self-discussion ; to debate in letters
Vext points with earnest friends ; past other men
To cherish natural instincts, yet to fear them
And less than any use them ; oh, no doubt,
In a corner sit and mope, and be consoled

With thinking one is clever, while the room
Rings through with animation and the dance.
Then talk of old examples ; to pervert
Ancient real facts to modern unreal dreams
And build up baseless fabrics of romance
And heroism upon historic sand ;
To burn, forsooth, for action, yet despise
Its merest accidence and alphabet ;
Cry out for service, and at once rebel
At the application of its plainest rules :
This you call life, my friend, reality ;
Doing your duty unto God and man—
I know not what.   Stay at Venice, if you will ;
Sit musing in its churches hour on hour
Cross-kneed upon a bench ; climb up at whiles
The neighbouring tower, and kill the lingering day
With old comparisons ; when night succeeds,
Evading, yet a little seeking, what
You would and would not, turn your doubtful eyes
On moon and stars to help morality ;
Once in a fortnight say, by lucky chance
Of happier-tempered coffee, gain (great Heaven !)
A pious rapture : is it not enough ?

Di.   'Tis well : thou cursed spirit, go thy way !
I am in higher hands than yours.

Sp.   'There is no God,' the wicked saith,
 'And truly it's a blessing,
For what He might have done with us
 It's better only guessing.'

'There is no God,' a youngster thinks,
 'Or really, if there may be,
He surely didn't mean a man
 Always to be a baby.'

'There is no God, or if there is,'
 The tradesman thinks, ' 'twere funny
If He should take it ill in me
 To make a little money.'

'Whether there be,' the rich man says,
 'It matters very little,
For I and mine, thank somebody,
 Are not in want of victual.'

Some others, also, to themselves,
 Who scarce so much as doubt it,
Think there is none, when they are well,
 And do not think about it.

But country folks who live beneath
 The shadow of the steeple ;
The parson and the parson's wife,
 And mostly married people ;

Youths green and happy in first love,
　　So thankful for illusion ;
And men caught out in what the world
　　Calls guilt, in first confusion ;

And almost every one when age,
　　Disease, or sorrows strike him,
Inclines to think there is a God,
　　Or something very like Him.

In a Gondola

Di. Afloat ; we move.　Delicious !　Ah,
What else is like the gondola ?
This level floor of liquid glass
Begins beneath us swift to pass.
It goes as though it went alone
By some impulsion of its own.
(How light it moves, how softly !　Ah,
Were all things like the gondola !)

How light it moves, how softly !　Ah,
Could life, as does our gondola,
Unvexed with quarrels, aims, and cares,
And moral duties and affairs,
Unswaying, noiseless, swift and strong,
For ever thus—thus glide along !
(How light we move, how softly !　Ah,
Were life but as the gondola !)

With no more motion than should bear
A freshness to the languid air ;
With no more effort than exprest
The need and naturalness of rest,
Which we beneath a grateful shade
Should take on peaceful pillows laid !
(How light we move, how softly !   Ah,
Were life but as the gondola !)

In one unbroken passage borne
To closing night from opening morn,
Uplift at whiles slow eyes to mark
Some palace front, some passing bark ;
Through windows catch the varying shore,
And hear the soft turns of the oar !
(How light we move, how softly !   Ah,
Were life but as the gondola !)

How light we go, how soft we skim,
And all in moonlight seem to swim !
The south side rises o'er our bark,
A wall impenetrably dark ;
The north is seen profusely bright ;
The water, is it shade or light ?
Say, gentle moon, which conquers now
The flood, those massy hulls, or thou ?
(How light we go, how softly !   Ah,
Were life but as the gondola !)

How light we go, how soft we skim,
And all in moonlight seem to swim !
In moonlight is it now, or shade ?
In planes of sure division made,

By angles sharp of palace walls
The clear light and the shadow falls ;
O sight of glory, sight of wonder !
Seen, a pictorial portent, under,
O great Rialto, the vast round
Of thy thrice-solid arch profound !
(How light we go, how softly !   Ah,
Life should be as the gondola !)

How light we go, how soft we skim,
And all in moonlight seem to swim !
Against bright clouds projected dark,
The white dome now, reclined I mark,
And, by o'er-brilliant lamps displayed,
The Doge's columns and arcade ;
Over still waters mildly come
The distant waters and the hum.
(How light we go, how softly !   Ah,
Life should be as the gondola !)

How light we go, how soft we skim,
And all in open moonlight swim !
Ah, gondolier, slow, slow, more slow !
We go ; but wherefore thus should go ?
Ah, let not muscle all too strong
Beguile, betray thee to our wrong !
On to the landing, onward.   Nay,
Sweet dream, a little longer stay !
On to the landing ; here.   And, ah !
Life is not as the gondola.

Sp. This world is very odd we see,
    We do not comprehend it;
But in one fact we all agree,
    God won't, and we can't mend it.

Being common sense, it can't be sin
    To take it as I find it;
The pleasure to take pleasure in;
    The pain, try not to mind it.

Di. O let me love my love unto myself alone,
And know my knowledge to the world unknown;
No witness to the vision call,
Beholding, unbeheld of all;
And worship thee, with thee withdrawn, apart,
Whoe'er, whate'er thou art,
Within the closest veil of mine own inmost heart.

Better it were, thou sayest, to consent,
Feast while we may, and live ere life be spent;
Close up clear eyes, and call the unstable sure,
The unlovely lovely, and the filthy pure;
In self-belyings, self-deceivings roll,
And lose in Action, Passion, Talk, the soul.

Nay, better far to mark off thus much air,
And call it heaven; place bliss and glory there;
Fix perfect homes in the unsubstantial sky,
And say, what is not, will be by and by;
What here exists not must exist elsewhere.

But play no tricks upon thy soul, O man ;
Let fact be fact, and life the thing it can.

Di. Where are the great, whom thou would'st
    wish to praise thee ?
Where are the pure, whom thou would'st choose to
    love thee ?
Where are the brave, to stand supreme above thee,
Whose high commands would cheer, whose chid-
    ings raise thee ?
    Seek, seeker, in thyself ; submit to find
    In the stones, bread, and life in the blank mind.

Spectator ab extra

Sp. As I sat at the café, I said to myself,
They may talk as they please about what they
    call pelf,
They may sneer as they like about eating and
    drinking,
But help it I cannot, I cannot help thinking,
    How pleasant it is to have money, heigh ho !
    How pleasant it is to have money.

I sit at my table *en grand seigneur*,
And when I have done, throw a crust to the poor ;
Not only the pleasure, one's self, of good living,
But also the pleasure of now and then giving.
    So pleasant it is to have money, heigh ho !
    So pleasant it is to have money.

It was but last winter I came up to town,
But already I'm getting a little renown ;
I make new acquaintance where'er I appear ;
I am not too shy, and have nothing to fear.
 So pleasant it is to have money, heigh ho !
 So pleasant it is to have money.

I drive through the streets, and I care not a d——n ;
The people they stare, and they ask who I am ;
And if I should chance to run over a cad,
I can pay for the damage if ever so bad.
 So pleasant it is to have money, heigh ho !
 So pleasant it is to have money.

We stroll to our box and look down on the pit,
And if it weren't low should be tempted to spit ;
We loll and we talk until people look up,
And when it's half over we go out to sup.
 So pleasant it is to have money, heigh ho !
 So pleasant it is to have money.

The best of the tables and the best of the fare—
And as for the others, the devil may care ;
It isn't our fault if they dare not afford
To sup like a prince and be drunk as a lord.
 So pleasant it is to have money, heigh ho !
 So pleasant it is to have money.

We sit at our tables and tipple champagne ;
Ere one bottle goes, comes another again ;
The waiters they skip and they scuttle about,
And the landlord attends us so civilly out.
 So pleasant it is to have money, heigh ho !
 So pleasant it is to have money.

It was but last winter I came up to town,
But already I'm getting a little renown ;
I get to good houses without much ado,
Am beginning to see the nobility too.
   So pleasant it is to have money, heigh ho !
   So pleasant it is to have money.

O dear ! what a pity they ever should lose it !
For they are the gentry that know how to use it ;
So grand and so graceful, such manners, such
     dinners,
But yet, after all, it is we are the winners.
   So pleasant it is to have money, heigh ho !
   So pleasant it is to have money.

Thus I sat at my table *en grand seigneur*,
And when I had done threw a crust to the poor ;
Not only the pleasure, one's self, of good eating,
But also the pleasure of now and then treating.
   So pleasant it is to have money, heigh ho !
   So pleasant it is to have money.

They may talk as they please about what they
     call pelf,
And how one ought never to think of one's self,
And how pleasures of thought surpass eating and
     drinking—
My pleasure of thought is the pleasure of thinking
   How pleasant it is to have money, heigh ho !
   How pleasant it is to have money.

Sp. Submit, submit!
'Tis common sense, and human wit
Can claim no higher name than it.
Submit, submit!
Devotion, and ideas, and love,
And beauty claim their place above;
But saint and sage and poet's dreams
Divide the light in coloured streams,
Which this alone gives all combined,
The *siccum lumen* of the mind
Called common sense: and no high wit
Gives better counsel than does it.
Submit, submit!

To see things simply as they are
Here at our elbows, transcends far
Trying to spy out at mid-day
Some 'bright particular star,' which may,
Or not, be visible at night,
But clearly is not in daylight;
No inspiration vague outweighs
The plain good common sense that says,
Submit, submit!
'Tis common sense, and human wit
Can ask no higher name than it.
Submit, submit!

Submit, submit!
For tell me then, in earth's great laws
Have you found any saving clause,

Exemption special granted you
From doing what the rest must do ?
Of common sense who made you quit,
And told you, you'd no need of it,
Nor to submit ?

This stern necessity of things
On every side our being rings ;
Our sallying eager actions fall
Vainly against that iron wall.
Where once her finger points the way,
The wise thinks only to obey ;
Take life as she has ordered it,
And come what may of it, submit,
Submit, submit !

Who take implicitly her will,
For these her vassal chances still
Bring store of joys, successes, pleasures ;
But whoso ponders, weighs, and measures,
She calls her torturers up to goad
With spur and scourges on the road ;
He does at last with pain whate'er
He spurned at first.   Of such, beware,
Beware, beware !

Necessity ! and who shall dare
Bring to *her* feet excuse or prayer ?
Beware, beware !
We must, we must.
Howe'er we turn, and pause and tremble—
Howe'er we shrink, deceive, dissemble—
Whate'er our doubting, grief, disgust,

The hand is on us, and we must,
We must, we must.
'Tis common sense ! and human wit
Can find no better name than
Submit, submit !

Di. When the enemy is near thee,
　　Call on us !
In our hands we will upbear thee,
He shall neither scathe nor scare thee,
He shall fly thee, and shall fear thee.
　　Call on us !
Call when all good friends have left thee,
Of all good sights and sounds bereft thee ;
Call when hope and heart are sinking,
And the brain is sick with thinking,
　　Help, O help !
Call, and following close behind thee
There shall haste, and there shall find thee,
　　Help, sure help.

When the panic comes upon thee,
When necessity seems on thee,
Hope and choice have all foregone thee,
Fate and force are closing o'er thee,
And but one way stands before thee—
　　Call on us !
Oh, and if thou dost not call,
Be but faithful, that is all.
Go right on, and close behind thee
There shall follow still and find thee,
　　Help, sure help.

FROM 'AMOURS DE VOYAGE'

FROM 'AMOURS DE VOYAGE'

Over the great windy waters, and over the clear-
crested summits,
   Unto the sun and the sky, and unto the perfecter
   earth,
Come, let us go,—to a land wherein gods of the
old time wandered,
   Where every breath even now changes to ether
   divine.
Come, let us go; though withal a voice whisper,
   ' The world that we live in,
   Whithersoever we turn, still is the same narrow
   crib;
'Tis but to prove limitation, and measure a cord,
that we travel;
   Let who would 'scape and be free go to his
   chamber and think;
'Tis but to change idle fancies for memories wilfully
   falser;
   'Tis but to go and have been.'—Come, little bark!
   let us go.

Claude to Eustace [1]

ROME disappoints me much ; I hardly as yet
  understand, but
Rubbishy seems the word that most exactly would
  suit it.
All the foolish destructions, and all the sillier
  savings,
All the incongruous things of past incompatible
  ages,
Seem to be treasured up here to make fools of
  present and future.
Would to Heaven the old Goths had made a
  cleaner sweep of it !
Would to Heaven some new ones would come and
  destroy these churches !
However, one can live in Rome as also in
  London.
It is a blessing, no doubt, to be rid, at least for
  a time, of
All one's friends and relations,—yourself (forgive
  me !) included,—
All the *assujettissement* of having been what one
  has been,
What one thinks one is, or thinks that others
  suppose one ;
Yet, in despite of all, we turn like fools to the
  English.

[1] The poem is in the form of letters from Claude the
traveller, in Rome, to his friend Eustace, in England.

No, great Dome of Agrippa, thou art not Christian !
    canst not,
Strip and replaster and daub and do what they
    will with thee, be so !
Here underneath the great porch of colossal
    Corinthian columns,
Here as I walk, do I dream of the Christian
    belfries above them ;
Or, on a bench as I sit and abide for long hours,
    till thy whole vast
Round grows dim as in dreams to my eyes, I
    repeople thy niches,
Not with the Martyrs, and Saints, and Confessors,
    and Virgins, and children,
But with the mightier forms of an older, austerer
    worship ;
And I recite to myself, how
                Eager for battle here
  Stood Vulcan, here matronal Juno,
    And with the bow to his shoulder faithful
  He who with pure dew laveth of Castaly
  His flowing locks, who holdeth of Lycia
  The oak forest and the wood that bore him,
  Delos' and Patara's own Apollo.[1]

> [1] Hic avidus stetit
>   Vulcanus, hic matrona Juno, et
>   Nunquam humeris positurus arcum ;
>   Qui rore puro Castaliæ lavit
>   Crines solutos, qui Lyciæ tenet
>   Dumeta natalemque silvam,
>   Delius et Patareus Apollo.

YET it is pleasant, I own it, to be in their company ;
    pleasant,
Whatever else it may be, to abide in the feminine
    presence.
Pleasant, but wrong, will you say?   But this
    happy, serene coexistence
Is to some poor soft souls, I fear, a necessity simple,
Meat and drink and life, and music, filling with
    sweetness,
Thrilling with melody sweet, with harmonies
    strange overwhelming,
All the long-silent strings of an awkward, meaning-
    less fabric.
Yet as for that, I could live, I believe, with
    children ; to have those
Pure and delicate forms encompassing, moving
    about you,
This were enough, I could think ; and truly with
    glad resignation
Could from the dream of Romance, from the fever
    of flushed adolescence,
Look to escape and subside into peaceful avuncular
    functions.
Nephews and nieces ! alas, for as yet I have none !
    and, moreover,
Mothers are jealous, I fear me, too often, too
    rightfully ; fathers
Think they have title exclusive to spoiling their
    own little darlings ;
And by the law of the land, in despite of Malthusian
    doctrine,

No sort of proper provision is made for that most
    patriotic,
Most meritorious subject, the childless and bachelor
    uncle.

YE, too, marvellous Twain, that erect on the Monte
    Cavallo
Stand by your rearing steeds in the grace of your
    motionless movement,
Stand with your upstretched arms and tranquil
    regardant faces,
Stand as instinct with life in the might of immut-
    able manhood,—
O ye mighty and strange, ye ancient divine ones
    of Hellas.
Are ye Christian too? to convert and redeem and
    renew you,
Will the brief form have sufficed, that a Pope has
    set up on the apex
Of the Egyptian stone that o'ertops you, the
    Christian symbol?
  And ye, silent, supreme in serene and victorious
    marble,
Ye that encircle the walls of the stately Vatican
    chambers,
Juno and Ceres, Minerva, Apollo, the Muses and
    Bacchus,
Ye unto whom far and near come posting the
    Christian pilgrims,
Ye that are ranged in the halls of the mystic
    Christian Pontiff,

Are ye also baptized ? are ye of the kingdom of
    Heaven ?
Utter, O some one, the word that shall reconcile
    Ancient and Modern !
Am I to turn me from this unto thee, great Chapel
    of Sixtus ?

I AM in love, meantime, you think ; no doubt you
    would think so.
I am in love, you say ; with those letters, of
    course, you would say so.
I am in love, you declare.   I think not so ; yet I
    grant you
It is a pleasure indeed to converse with this girl.
    Oh, rare gift,
Rare felicity, this ! she can talk in a rational way,
    can
Speak upon subjects that really are matters of
    mind and of thinking,
Yet in perfection retain her simplicity ; never, one
    moment,
Never, however you urge it, however you tempt
    her, consents to
Step from ideas and fancies and loving sensations
    to those vain
Conscious understandings that vex the minds of
    mankind.
No, though she talk, it is music ; her fingers desert
    not the keys ; 'tis
Song, though you hear in the song the articulate
    vocables sounded,

Syllabled singly and sweetly the words of melodious
    meaning.
  I am in love, you say: I do not think so,
    exactly.

THERE are two different kinds, I believe, of human
    attraction ;
One which simply disturbs, unsettles, and makes
    you uneasy,
And another that poises, retains, and fixes and
    holds you.
I have no doubt, for myself, in giving my voice
    for the latter.
I do not wish to be moved, but growing where I
    was growing,
There more truly to grow, to live where as yet I
    had languished.
I do not like being moved : for the will is excited ;
    and action
Is a most dangerous thing ; I tremble for some-
    thing factitious,
Some malpractice of heart and illegitimate
    process ;
We are so prone to these things, with our terrible
    notions of duty.

AH, let me look, let me watch, let me wait, un-
hurried, unprompted !
Bid me not venture on aught that could alter or
end what is present !
Say not, Time flies, and Occasion, that never
returns, is departing !
Drive me not out, ye ill angels with fiery swords,
from my Eden,
Waiting, and watching, and looking !   Let love
be its own inspiration !
Shall not a voice, if a voice there must be, from
the airs that environ,
Yea, from the conscious heavens, without our
knowledge or effort,
Break into audible words ?   And love be its own
inspiration ?

JUXTAPOSITION, in fine ; and what is juxtaposition ?
Look you, we travel along in the railway-carriage
or steamer,
And, *pour passer le temps*, till the tedious journey
be ended,
Lay aside paper or book, to talk with the girl that
is next one ;
And, *pour passer le temps*, with the terminus all
but in prospect,
Talk of eternal ties and marriages made in heaven.
    Ah, did we really accept with a perfect heart
the illusion !

Ah, did we really believe that the Present indeed
   is the Only !
Or through all transmutation, all shock and
   convulsion of passion,
Feel we could carry undimmed, unextinguished,
   the light of our knowledge !
  But for his funeral train which the bridegroom
   sees in the distance,
Would he so joyfully, think you, fall in with the
   marriage procession ?
But for that final discharge, would he dare to
   enlist in that service ?
But for that certain release, ever sign to that
   perilous contract ?
But for that exit secure, ever bend to that
   treacherous doorway ?—
Ah, but the bride, meantime,—do you think she
   sees it as he does ?
  But for the steady fore-sense of a freer and
   larger existence,
Think you that man could consent to be circum-
   scribed here into action ?
But for assurance within of a limitless ocean
   divine, o'er
Whose great tranquil depths unconscious the
   wind-tost surface
Breaks into ripples of trouble that come and
   change and endure not,—
But that in this, of a truth, we have our being,
   and know it,
Think you we men could submit to live and move
   as we do here ?

Ah, but the women,—God bless them! they don't
    think at all about it.
  Yet we must eat and drink, as you say.   And
    as limited beings
Scarcely can hope to attain upon earth to an
    Actual Abstract,
Leaving to God contemplation, to His hands
    knowledge confiding,
Sure that in us if it perish, in Him it abideth and
    dies not,
Let us in His sight accomplish our petty particular
    doings,—
Yes, and contented sit down to the victual that
    He has provided.
Allah is great, no doubt, and Juxtaposition his
    prophet.
Ah, but the women, alas! they don't look at it in
    that way.
Juxtaposition is great;—but, my friend, I fear me,
    the maiden
Hardly would thank or acknowledge the lover
    that sought to obtain her,
Not as the thing he would wish, but the thing he
    must even put up with,—
Hardly would tender her hand to the wooer that
    candidly told her
That she is but for a space, an *ad-interim* solace
    and pleasure,—
That in the end she shall yield to a perfect and
    absolute something,
Which I then for myself shall behold, and not
    another,—

Which amid fondest endearments, meantime I
forget not, forsake not.
Ah, ye feminine souls, so loving, and so exacting,
Since we cannot escape, must we even submit to
deceive you ?
Since, so cruel is truth, sincerity shocks and
revolts you,
Will you have us your slaves to lie to you, flatter
and—leave you ?

TIBUR is beautiful, too, and the orchard slopes,
and the Anio
Falling, falling yet, to the ancient lyrical cadence ;
Tibur, and Anio's tide ; and cool from Lucretilis
ever,
With the Digentian stream, and with the Bandu-
sian fountain,
Folded in Sabine recesses, the valley and villa of
Horace :—
So not seeing I sang ; so seeing and listening say
I,
Here as I sit by the stream, as I gaze at the cell
of the Sibyl,
Here with Albunea's home and the grove of
Tiburnus beside me ;[1]
Tivoli beautiful is, and musical, O Teverone,
Dashing from mountain to plain, thy parted
impetuous waters,

[1] —— domus Albuneæ resonantis,
Et præceps Anio, et Tiburni lucus, et uda
Mobilibus pomaria rivis.

Tivoli's waters and rocks ; and fair unto Monte
   Gennaro
(Haunt, even yet, I must think, as I wander and
   gaze, of the shadows,
Faded and pale, yet immortal, of Faunus, the
   Nymphs, and the Graces),
Fair in itself, and yet fairer with human completing
   creations,
Folded in Sabine recesses the valley and villa of
   Horace :—
So not seeing I sang ; so now—Nor seeing, nor
   hearing,
Neither by waterfall lulled, nor folded in sylvan
   embraces,
Neither by cell of the Sibyl, nor stepping the
   Monte Gennaro,
Seated on Anio's bank, nor sipping Bandusian
   waters,
But on Montorio's height, looking down on the
   tile-clad streets, the
Cupolas, crosses, and domes, the bushes and
   kitchen-gardens,
Which, by the grace of the Tibur, proclaim them-
   selves Rome of the Romans,—
But on Montorio's height, looking forth to the
   vapoury mountains,
Cheating the prisoner Hope with illusions of vision
   and fancy,—
But on Montorio's height, with these weary
   soldiers by me,
Waiting till Oudinot enter, to reinstate Pope and
   Tourist.

WHITHER depart the souls of the brave that die
    in the battle,
Die in the lost, lost fight, for the cause that
    perishes with them?
Are they upborne from the field on the slumberous
    pinions of angels
Unto a far-off home, where the weary rest from
    their labour,
And the deep wounds are healed, and the bitter
    and burning moisture
Wiped from the generous eyes? or do they linger,
    unhappy,
Pining, and haunting the grave of their bygone
    hope and endeavour?

SHALL we come out of it all, some day, as one
    does from a tunnel?
Will it be all at once, without our doing or asking,
We shall behold clear day, the trees and meadows
    about us,
And the faces of friends, and the eyes we loved
    looking at us?
Who knows? Who can say? It will not do to
    suppose it.

Therefore farewell, ye hills, and ye, ye envine-
    yarded ruins!
    Therefore farewell, ye walls, palaces, pillars,
    and domes!
Therefore farewell, far seen, ye peaks of the mythic
    Albano,
    Seen from Montorio's height, Tibur and Æsula's
    hills!
Ah, could we once, ere we go, could we stand,
    while, to ocean descending,
    Sinks o'er the yellow dark plain slowly the
    yellow broad sun,
Stand, from the forest emerging at sunset, at once
    in the champaign,
    Open, but studded with trees, chestnuts um-
    brageous and old,
E'en in those fair open fields that incurve to thy
    beautiful hollow,
    Nemi, imbedded in wood, Nemi, inurned in the
    hill!—
Therefore farewell, ye plains, and ye hills, and
    the City Eternal!
    Therefore farewell! We depart, but to behold
    you again!

MISCELLANEOUS POEMS

'WITH WHOM IS NO VARIABLENESS, NEITHER SHADOW OF TURNING'

IT fortifies my soul to know
That, though I perish, Truth is so :
That, howsoe'er I stray and range,
Whate'er I do, Thou dost not change.
I steadier step when I recall
That, if I slip, Thou dost not fall.

THE LATEST DECALOGUE

THOU shalt have one God only; who
Would be at the expense of two?
No graven images may be
Worshipped, except the currency:
Swear not at all; for, for thy curse
Thine enemy is none the worse:
At church on Sunday to attend
Will serve to keep the world thy friend:
Honour thy parents; that is, all
From whom advancement may befall:
Thou shalt not kill; but need'st not strive
Officiously to keep alive:
Do not adultery commit;
Advantage rarely comes of it:
Thou shalt not steal; an empty feat,
When it's so lucrative to cheat:
Bear not false witness; let the lie
Have time on its own wings to fly:
Thou shalt not covet, but tradition
Approves all forms of competition.

HOPE EVERMORE AND BELIEVE

HOPE evermore and believe, O man, for e'en as
   thy thought
  So are the things that thou see'st ; e'en as thy
  hope and belief.
Cowardly art thou and timid ? they rise to provoke
  thee against them ;
  Hast thou courage ? enough, see them exulting
  to yield.
Yea, the rough rock, the dull earth, the cold sea's
   furying waters
  (Violent, say'st thou and hard, mighty thou
  think'st to destroy),
All with ineffable longing are waiting their Invader,
  All, with one varying voice, call to him, Come
  and subdue ;
Still for their Conqueror call, and, but for the joy
  of being conquered
  (Rapture they would not forego), dare to resist
  and rebel ;
Still, when resisting and raging, in soft under-voice
  say unto him,
  Fear not, retire not, O man : hope evermore
  and believe.

Go from the east to the west, as the sun and the
    stars direct thee,
    Go, with the girdle of man, go and encompass
    the earth.
Not for the gain of the gold ; for the getting, the
    hoarding, the having,
    But for the joy of the deed ; but for the duty
    to do.
Go with the spiritual life, the higher volition and
    action,
    With the great girdle of God, go and encompass
    the earth.

Go ; say not in thy heart, And what then were it
    accomplished,
    Were the wild impulse allayed, what were the use
    or the good !
Go, when the instinct is stilled, and when the deed
    is accomplished,
    What thou hast done and shalt do, shall be
    declared to thee then.
Go with the sun and the stars, and yet evermore
    in thy spirit
    Say to thyself : It is good : yet is there better
    than it.
This that I see is not all, and this that I do is but
    little ;
    Nevertheless it is good, though there is better
    than it.

'THROUGH A GLASS DARKLY'

WHAT we, when face to face we see
The Father of our souls, shall be,
John tells us, doth not yet appear ;
Ah ! did he tell what we are here !

A mind for thoughts to pass into,
A heart for loves to travel through,
Five senses to detect things near,
Is this the whole that we are here ?

Rules baffle instincts—instincts rules,
Wise men are bad—and good are fools,
Facts evil—wishes vain appear,
We cannot go, why are we here ?

O may we for assurance' sake,
Some arbitrary judgment take,
And wilfully pronounce it clear,
For this or that 'tis we are here ?

Or is it right, and will it do,
To pace the sad confusion through,
And say :—It doth not yet appear,
What we shall be, what we are here ?

N

Ah yet, when all is thought and said,
The heart still overrules the head ;
Still what we hope we must believe,
And what is given us receive ;

Must still believe, for still we hope
That in a world of larger scope,
What here is faithfully begun
Will be completed, not undone.

AH ! YET CONSIDER IT AGAIN !

'OLD things need not be therefore true,'
O brother men, nor yet the new ;
Ah ! still awhile the old thought retain,
And yet consider it again !

The souls of now two thousand years
Have laid up here their toils and fears,
And all the earnings of their pain,—
Ah, yet consider it again !

We ! what do we see ? each a space
Of some few yards before his face ;
Does that the whole wide plan explain ?
Ah, yet consider it again !

Alas ! the great world goes its way,
And takes its truth from each new day ;
They do not quit, nor can retain,
Far less consider it again.

1851

ITE DOMUM SATURÆ, VENIT HESPERUS

THE skies have sunk, and hid the upper snow
(Home, Rose, and home, Provence and La Palie),
The rainy clouds are filing fast below,
And wet will be the path, and wet shall we.
Home, Rose, and home, Provence and La Palie.

Ah dear, and where is he, a year agone,
Who stepped beside and cheered us on and on?
My sweetheart wanders far away from me,
In foreign land or on a foreign sea.
Home, Rose, and home, Provence and La Palie.

The lightning zigzags shoot across the sky
(Home, Rose, and home, Provence and La Palie),
And through the vale the rains go sweeping by;
Ah me, and when in shelter shall we be?
Home, Rose, and home, Provence and La Palie.

Cold, dreary cold, the stormy winds feel they
O'er foreign lands and foreign seas that stray
(Home, Rose, and home, Provence and La Palie).
And doth he e'er, I wonder, bring to mind
The pleasant huts and herds he left behind?

And doth he sometimes in his slumbering see
The feeding kine, and doth he think of me,
My sweetheart wandering wheresoe'er it be?
Home, Rose, and home, Provence and La Palie.

The thunder bellows far from snow to snow
(Home, Rose, and home, Provence and La Palie),
And loud and louder roars the flood below.
Heigho! but soon in shelter shall we be:
Home, Rose, and home, Provence and La Palie.

Or shall he find before his term be sped,
Some comelier maid that he shall wish to wed?
(Home, Rose, and home, Provence and La Palie.)
For weary is work, and weary day by day
To have your comfort miles on miles away.
Home, Rose, and home, Provence and La Palie.

Or may it be that I shall find my mate,
And he returning see himself too late?
For work we must, and what we see, we see,
And God he knows, and what must be, must be,
When sweethearts wander far away from me.
Home, Rose, and home, Provence and La Palie.

The sky behind is brightening up anew
(Home, Rose, and home, Provence and La Palie),
The rain is ending, and our journey too:
Heigho! aha! for here at home are we:—
In, Rose, and in, Provence and La Palie.

A LONDON IDYLL

ON grass, on gravel, in the sun,
  Or now beneath the shade,
They went, in pleasant Kensington,
  A prentice and a maid.
That Sunday morning's April glow,
  How should it not impart
A stir about the veins that flow
  To feed the youthful heart.

> Ah ! years may come, and years may bring
>   The truth that is not bliss,
> But will they bring another thing
>   That can compare with this ?

I read it in that arm she lays
  So soft on his ; her mien,
Her step, her very gown betrays
  (What in her eyes were seen)
That not in vain the young buds round,
  The cawing birds above,
The air, the incense of the ground,
  Are whispering, breathing love.

> Ah ! years may come, etc.

To inclination, young and blind,
   So perfect, as they lent,
By purest innocence confined
   Unconscious free consent.
Persuasive power of vernal change,
   On this, thine earliest day,
Canst thou have found in all thy range
   One fitter type than they?

     Ah! years may come, etc.

Th' high-titled cares of adult strife,
   Which we our duties call,
Trades, arts, and politics of life,
   Say, have they after all,
One other object, end or use
   Than that, for girl and boy,
The punctual earth may still produce
   This golden flower of joy?

     Ah! years may come, etc.

O odours of new-budding rose,
   O lily's chaste perfume,
O fragrance that didst first unclose
   The young Creation's bloom!
Ye hang around me, while in sun
   Anon and now in shade,
I watched in pleasant Kensington
   The prentice and the maid.

     Ah! years may come, and years may bring
       The truth that is not bliss,
      But will they bring another thing
       That will compare with this?

THE STREAM OF LIFE

O STREAM descending to the sea,
  Thy mossy banks between,
The flow'rets blow, the grasses grow,
  The leafy trees are green.

In garden plots the children play,
  The fields the labourers till,
And houses stand on either hand,
  And thou descendest still.

O life descending into death,
  Our waking eyes behold,
Parent and friend thy lapse attend,
  Companions young and old.

Strong purposes our mind possess,
  Our hearts affections fill,
We toil and earn, we seek and learn,
  And thou descendest still.

O end to which our currents tend,
  Inevitable sea,
To which we flow, what do we know,
  What shall we guess of thee ?

A roar we hear upon thy shore,
  As we our course fulfil ;
Scarce we divine a sun will shine
  And be above us still.

IN A LONDON SQUARE

PUT forth thy leaf, thou lofty plane,
  East wind and frost are safely gone ;
With zephyr mild and balmy rain
  The summer comes serenely on ;
Earth, air, and sun and skies combine
  To promise all that's kind and fair :—
But thou, O human heart of mine,
  Be still, contain thyself, and bear.

December days were brief and chill,
  The winds of March were wild and drear,
And, nearing and receding still,
  Spring never would, we thought, be here.
The leaves that burst, the suns that shine,
  Had, not the less, their certain date :—
And thou, O human heart of mine,
  Be still, refrain thyself, and wait.

THE SHADOW [1]

I DREAMED a dream: I dreamt that I espied,
Upon a stone that was not rolled aside,
A Shadow sit upon a grave—a Shade,
As thin, as unsubstantial, as of old
Came, the Greek poet told,
To lick the life-blood in the trench Ulysses made—
As pale, as thin, and said:
'I am the Resurrection of the Dead.
The night is past, the morning is at hand,
And I must in my proper semblance stand,
Appear brief space and vanish,—listen, this is true,
I am that Jesus whom they slew.'

And shadows dim, I dreamed, the dead apostles
      came,
And bent their heads for sorrow and for shame—
Sorrow for their great loss, and shame
For what they did in that vain name.

And in long ranges far behind there seemed
Pale vapoury angel forms; 'or was it cloud? that
      kept
Strange watch; the women also stood beside and
      wept.

---

[1] The manuscript of this poem is incomplete.

And Peter spoke the word :
' O my own Lord,
What is it we must do ?
Is it then all untrue ?
Did we not see, and hear, and handle Thee,
Yea, for whole hours
Upon the Mount in Galilee,
On the lake shore, and here at Bethany,
When Thou ascendedst to Thy God and ours ? '
   And paler still became the distant cloud,
And at the word the women wept aloud.

And the Shade answered, ' What ye say I know
      not ;
            But it is true
            I am that Jesus whom they slew,
Whom ye have preached, but in what way I know
      not.'

         .   .   .   .   .

And the great World, it chanced, came by that
      way,
And stopped, and looked, and spoke to the police,
And said the thing, for order's sake and peace,
Most certainly must be suppressed, the nuisance
      cease.
His wife and daughter must have where to pray,
And whom to pray to, at the least one day
In seven, and something sensible to say.

Whether the fact so many years ago
Had, or not, happened, how was he to know ?
Yet he had always heard that it was so.
As for himself, perhaps it was all one ;

And yet he found it not unpleasant, too,
On Sunday morning in the roomy pew,
To see the thing with such decorum done.
As for himself, perhaps it was all one ;
Yet on one's death-bed all men always said
It was a comfortable thing to think upon
The atonement and the resurrection of the dead.
So the great World as having said his say,
Unto his country-house pursued his way.
And on the grave the Shadow sat all day.

EASTER DAY

NAPLES, 1849

THROUGH the great sinful streets of Naples as I
    past,
  With fiercer heat than flamed above my head
My heart was hot within me ; till at last
  My brain was lightened when my tongue had
    said—
        Christ is not risen !

    Christ is not risen, no—
      He lies and moulders low ;
    Christ is not risen !

What though the stone were rolled away, and
    though
    The grave found empty there ?—
    If not there, then elsewhere ;
If not where Joseph laid Him first, why then
    Where other men
Translaid Him after, in some humbler clay.
    Long ere to-day
Corruption that sad perfect work hath done,
Which here she scarcely, lightly had begun :
    The foul engendered worm
Feeds on the flesh of the life-giving form

Of our most Holy and Anointed One.
  He is not risen, no—
  He lies and moulders low ;
   Christ is not risen !

What if the women, ere the dawn was grey,
Saw one or more great angels, as they say
(Angels, or Him Himself) ?   Yet neither there,
  nor then,
Nor afterwards, nor elsewhere, nor at all,
Hath He appeared to Peter or the Ten ;
Nor, save in thunderous terror, to blind Saul ;
Save in an after Gospel and late Creed,
  He is not risen, indeed,—
   Christ is not risen !

Or, what if e'en, as runs a tale, the Ten
Saw, heard, and touched, again and yet again ?
What if at Emmaüs' inn, and by Capernaum's
  Lake,
  Came One, the bread that brake—
Came One that spake as never mortal spake,
And with them ate, and drank, and stood, and
  walked about ?
  Ah ! 'some' did well to 'doubt' !
Ah ! the true Christ, while these things came to
  pass,
Nor heard, nor spake, nor walked, nor lived, alas !
  He was not risen, no—
  He lay and mouldered low,
   Christ was not risen !

As circulates in some great city crowd
A rumour changeful, vague, importunate, and loud,
From no determined centre, or of fact
    Or authorship exact,
    Which no man can deny
      Nor verify;
    So spread the wondrous fame;
    He all the same
    Lay senseless, mouldering, low:
    He was not risen, no—
      Christ was not risen!

Ashes to ashes, dust to dust;
As of the unjust, also of the just—
    Yea, of that Just One, too!
This is the one sad Gospel that is true—
    Christ is not risen!

Is He not risen, and shall we not rise?
    Oh, we unwise!
What did we dream, what wake we to discover?
Ye hills, fall on us, and ye mountains, cover!
    In darkness and great gloom
Come ere we thought it is *our* day of doom;
From the cursed world, which is one tomb,
    Christ is not risen!

Eat, drink, and play, and think that this is bliss:
There is no heaven but this;
    There is no hell,
Save earth, which serves the purpose doubly well,
    Seeing it visits still
With equallest apportionment of ill

Both good and bad alike, and brings to one same
  dust
   The unjust and the just
   With Christ, who is not risen.

Eat, drink, and die, for we are souls bereaved :
  Of all the creatures under heaven's wide cope
  We are most hopeless, who had once most hope,
And most beliefless, that had most believed.
   Ashes to ashes, dust to dust ;
   As of the unjust, also of the just—
   Yea, of that Just One too !
   It is the one sad Gospel that is true—
    Christ is not risen !

   Weep not beside the tomb,
   Ye women, unto whom
He was great solace while ye tended Him ;
   Ye who with napkin o'er the head
And folds of linen round each wounded limb
   Laid out the Sacred Dead ;
And thou that bar'st Him in thy wondering womb;
Yea, Daughters of Jerusalem, depart,
Bind up as best ye may your own sad bleeding
  heart :
Go to your homes, your living children tend,
   Your earthly spouses love ;
   Set your affections *not* on things above,
Which moth and rust corrupt, which quickliest
  come to end :
Or pray, if pray ye must, and pray, if pray ye can,
For death ; since dead is He whom ye deemed
  more than man,

Who is not risen : no—
But lies and moulders low—
    Who is not risen !

    Ye men of Galilee !
Why stand ye looking up to heaven, where Him
    ye ne'er may see,
Neither ascending hence, nor returning hither
    again ?
    Ye ignorant and idle fishermen !
Hence to your huts, and boats, and inland native
    shore,
    And catch not men, but fish ;
    Whate'er things ye might wish,
Him neither here nor there ye e'er shall meet with
    more.
    Ye poor deluded youths, go home,
    Mend the old nets ye left to roam,
    Tie the split oar, patch the torn sail :
    It was indeed an ' idle tale '—
    He was not risen !

And, oh, good men of ages yet to be,
Who shall believe *because* ye did not see—
    Oh, be ye warned, be wise !
    No more with pleading eyes,
    And sobs of strong desire,
    Unto the empty vacant void aspire,
Seeking another and impossible birth
That is not of your own, and only mother earth.
But if there is no other life for you,
Sit down and be content, since this must even do :
    He is not risen !

O

One look, and then depart,
　　Ye humble and ye holy men of heart ;
And ye ! ye ministers and stewards of a Word
Which ye would preach, because another heard—
　　Ye worshippers of that ye do not know,
　　Take these things hence and go :—
　　He is not risen !

　　Here, on our Easter Day
We rise, we come, and lo ! we find Him not,
Gardener nor other, on the sacred spot :
Where they have laid Him there is none to say ;
No sound, nor in, nor out—no word
Of where to seek the dead or meet the living Lord.
There is no glistering of an angel's wings,
There is no voice of heavenly clear behest :
Let us go hence, and think upon these things
　　In silence, which is best.
　　Is He not risen ?   No—
　　But lies and moulders low ?
　　Christ is not risen ?

EASTER DAY

II

So in the sinful streets, abstracted and alone,
I with my secret self held communing of mine
    own.
  So in the southern city spake the tongue
Of one that somewhat overwildly sung,
But in a later hour I sat and heard
Another voice that spake—another graver word.
Weep not, it bade, whatever hath been said,
Though He be dead, He is not dead.
      In the true creed
      He is yet risen indeed ;
        Christ is yet risen.

Weep not beside His tomb,
Ye women unto whom
He was great comfort and yet greater grief ;
Nor ye, ye faithful few that wont with Him to
    roam,
Seek sadly what for Him ye left, go hopeless to
    your home ;
Nor ye despair, ye sharers yet to be of their belief;
      Though He be dead, He is not dead,
      Nor gone, though fled,
      Not lost, though vanished ;

Though He return not, though
He lies and moulders low ;
In the true creed
He is yet risen indeed ;
  Christ is yet risen.

Sit if ye will, sit down upon the ground,
Yet not to weep and wail, but calmly look around.
  Whate'er befell,
  Earth is not hell ;
Now, too, as when it first began,
Life is yet life, and man is man.
For all that breathe beneath the heaven's high
    cope,
Joy with grief mixes, with despondence hope.
Hope conquers cowardice, joy grief :
Or at least, faith unbelief.
  Though dead, not dead ;
  Not gone, though fled ;
  Not lost, though vanished.
  In the great gospel and true creed,
  He is yet risen indeed ;
    Christ is yet risen.

PESCHIERA

WHAT voice did on my spirit fall,
Peschiera, when thy bridge I crost?
' 'Tis better to have fought and lost,
Than never to have fought at all.'

The tricolor—a trampled rag
Lies, dirt and dust; the lines I track
By sentry boxes yellow-black,
Lead up to no Italian flag.

I see the Croat soldier stand
Upon the grass of your redoubts;
The eagle with his black wings flouts
The breath and beauty of your land.

Yet not in vain, although in vain,
O men of Brescia, on the day
Of loss past hope, I heard you say
Your welcome to the noble pain.

You say, ' Since so it is,—good-bye
Sweet life, high hope; but whatsoe'er
May be, or must, no tongue shall dare
To tell, " The Lombard feared to die!"'

You said (there shall be answer fit),
'And if our children must obey,
They must ; but thinking on this day
'Twill less debase them to submit.'

You said (Oh not in vain you said),
' Haste, brothers, haste, while yet we may ;
The hours ebb fast of this one day
When blood may yet be nobly shed.'

Ah ! not for idle hatred, not
For honour, fame, nor self-applause,
But for the glory of the cause,
You did, what will not be forgot.

And though the stranger stand, 'tis true,
By force and fortune's right he stands ;
By fortune, which is in God's hands,
And strength, which yet shall spring in you.

This voice did on my spirit fall,
Peschiera, when thy bridge I crost,
' 'Tis better to have fought and lost,
Than never to have fought at all.'

1849

SAY NOT THE STRUGGLE NOUGHT AVAILETH

SAY not the struggle nought availeth,
  The labour and the wounds are vain,
The enemy faints not, nor faileth,
  And as things have been they remain.

If hopes were dupes, fears may be liars ;
  It may be, in yon smoke concealed,
Your comrades chase e'en now the fliers,
  And, but for you, possess the field.

For while the tired waves, vainly breaking,
  Seem here no painful inch to gain,
Far back, through creeks and inlets making,
  Comes silent, flooding in, the main,

And not by eastern windows only,
  When daylight comes, comes in the light,
In front, the sun climbs slow, how slowly,
  But westward, look, the land is bright.

1849

SONGS WRITTEN ON SHIP-BOARD [1]

FAREWELL, farewell! Her vans the vessel tries,
His iron might the potent engine plies ;
Haste, wingèd words, and ere 'tis useless, tell,
Farewell, farewell, yet once again, farewell.

The docks, the streets, the houses past us fly,
Without a strain the great ship marches by ;
Ye fleeting banks take up the words we tell,
And say for us yet once again, farewell.

The waters widen—on without a strain
The strong ship moves upon the open main ;
She knows the seas, she hears the true waves swell,
She seems to say farewell, again farewell.

The billows whiten and the deep seas heave ;
Fly once again, sweet words, to her I leave,
With winds that blow return, and seas that swell,
Farewell, farewell, say once again, farewell.

Fresh in my face and rippling to my feet
The winds and waves an answer soft repeat,

---

[1] This group of songs was composed during the writer's voyage across the Atlantic in 1852.

In sweet, sweet words far brought they seem to tell,
Farewell, farewell, yet once again, farewell.

Night gathers fast ; adieu, thou fading shore !
The land we look for next must lie before ;
Hence, foolish tears ! weak thoughts, no more rebel,
Farewell, farewell, a last, a last farewell.

Yet not, indeed, ah not till more than sea
And more than space divide my love and me,
Till more than waves and winds between us swell,
Farewell, a last, indeed, a last farewell.

COME home, come home ! and where is home for
    me,
Whose ship is driving o'er the trackless sea ?
To the frail bark here plunging on its way,
To the wild waters, shall I turn and say
To the plunging bark, or to the salt sea foam,
      You are my home ?

Fields once I walked in, faces once I knew,
Familiar things so old my heart believed them true,
These far, far back, behind me lie, before
The dark clouds mutter, and the deep seas roar,
And speak to them that 'neath and o'er them roam
      No words of home.

Beyond the clouds, beyond the waves that roar,
There may indeed, or may not be, a shore,

Where fields as green, and hands and hearts as
    true,
The old forgotten semblance may renew,
And offer exiles driven far o'er the salt sea foam
    Another home.

But toil and pain must wear out many a day,
And days bear weeks, and weeks bear months away,
Ere, if at all, the weary traveller hear,
With accents whispered in his wayworn ear,
A voice he dares to listen to, say, Come
    To thy true home.

Come home, come home! and where a home hath
    he
Whose ship is driving o'er the driving sea?
Through clouds that mutter, and o'er waves that
    roar,
Say, shall we find, or shall we not, a shore
That is, as is not ship or ocean foam,
    Indeed our home?

1852

_____

GREEN fields of England! wheresoe'er
Across this watery waste we fare,
Your image at our hearts we bear,
Green fields of England, everywhere.

Sweet eyes in England, I must flee
Past where the waves' last confines be,
Ere your loved smile I cease to see,
Sweet eyes in England, dear to me.

Dear home in England, safe and fast
If but in thee my lot lie cast,
The past shall seem a nothing past
To thee, dear home, if won at last ;
Dear home in England, won at last.

1852

———————

Come back, come back, behold with straining mast
And swelling sail, behold her steaming fast ;
With one new sun to see her voyage o'er,
With morning light to touch her native shore.
     Come back, come back.

Come back, come back, while westward labouring
    by,
With sailless yards, a bare black hulk we fly.
See how the gale we fight with sweeps her back,
To our lost home, on our forsaken track.
     Come back, come back.

Come back, come back, across the flying foam,
We hear faint far-off voices call us home,
Come back, ye seem to say ; ye seek in vain ;
We went, we sought, and homeward turned again.
     Come back, come back.

Come back, come back ; and whither back or why ?
To fan quenched hopes, forsaken schemes to try ;
Walk the old fields ; pace the familiar street ;
Dream with the idlers, with the bards compete.
     Come back, come back.

Come back, come back ; and whither and for what ?
To finger idly some old Gordian knot,
Unskilled to sunder, and too weak to cleave,
And with much toil attain to half-believe.
      Come back, come back.

Come back, come back ; yea back, indeed, do go
Sighs panting thick, and tears that want to flow ;
Fond fluttering hopes upraise their useless wings,
And wishes idly struggle in the strings ;
      Come back, come back.

Come back, come back, more eager than the breeze,
The flying fancies sweep across the seas,
And lighter far than ocean's flying foam,
The heart's fond message hurries to its home.
      Come back, come back.

Come back, come back !
Back flies the foam ; the hoisted flag streams back ;
The long smoke wavers on the homeward track,
Back fly with winds things which the winds obey,
The strong ship follows its appointed way.

1852

———————

Some future day when what is now is not,
When all old faults and follies are forgot,
And thoughts of difference passed like dreams
    away,
We'll meet again, upon some future day.

When all that hindered, all that vexed our love,
As tall rank weeds will climb the blade above,
When all but it has yielded to decay,
We'll meet again upon some future day.

When we have proved, each on his course alone,
The wider world, and learnt what's now unknown,
Have made life clear, and worked out each a way,
We'll meet again,—we shall have much to say.

With happier mood, and feelings born anew,
Our boyhood's bygone fancies we'll review,
Talk o'er old talks, play as we used to play,
And meet again, on many a future day.

Some day, which oft our hearts shall yearn to see,
In some far year, though distant yet to be,
Shall we indeed,—ye winds and waters, say!—
Meet yet again, upon some future day?

    1852

WHERE lies the land to which the ship would go?
Far, far ahead, is all her seamen know.
And where the land she travels from? Away,
Far, far behind, is all that they can say.

On sunny noons upon the deck's smooth face,
Linked arm in arm, how pleasant here to pace;
Or, o'er the stern reclining, watch below
The foaming wake far widening as we go.

On stormy nights when wild north-westers rave,
How proud a thing to fight with wind and wave !
The dripping sailor on the reeling mast
Exults to bear, and scorns to wish it past.

Where lies the land to which the ship would go ?
Far, far ahead, is all her seamen know.
And where the land she travels from ?   Away,
Far, far behind, is all that they can say.

1852

COME, POET, COME!

COME, Poet, come!
A thousand labourers ply their task,
And what it tends to scarcely ask,
And trembling thinkers on the brink
Shiver, and know not how to think.
To tell the purport of their pain,
And what our silly joys contain;
In lasting lineaments pourtray
The substance of the shadowy day;
Our real and inner deeds rehearse,
And make our meaning clear in verse:
Come, Poet, come! for but in vain
We do the work or feel the pain,
And gather up the seeming gain,
Unless before the end thou come
To take, ere they are lost, their sum.

Come, Poet, come!
To give an utterance to the dumb,
And make vain babblers silent, come;
A thousand dupes point here and there,
Bewildered by the show and glare;
And wise men half have learned to doubt
Whether we are not best without.
Come, Poet; both but wait to see
Their error proved to them in thee.

Come, Poet, come !
In vain I seem to call.   And yet
Think not the living times forget.
Ages of heroes fought and fell
That Homer in the end might tell ;
O'er grovelling generations past
Upstood the Doric fane at last ;
And countless hearts on countless years
Had wasted thoughts, and hopes, and fears,
Rude laughter and unmeaning tears ;
Ere England Shakespeare saw, or Rome
The pure perfection of her dome.
Others, I doubt not, if not we,
The issue of our toils shall see ;
Young children gather as their own
The harvest that the dead had sown,
The dead forgotten and unknown.

THE END